THE GOLDEN LOCKET
THE OBSIDIAN SPINDLE SAGA
BOOK ELEVEN

RUSSELL NOHELTY

SPECIAL THANKS

Talinda Willard, HyliaKumatora, Chris Roeszler, Amy Teegan, Chip Orlikowski, RHR, Victoria Nohelty, Alexander Joyner, Pierino Gattei, Caspar Williams, Gerald P. McDaniel, Walter Weiss, Sunny Side Up, Kenny Endlich, Amber Reeves, Joshua Bowers, Elias Rosner, Noah Carruba, John "AcesofDeath7" Mullens, Jamie Minnich, Rowan Stone, Taiga Char, BAOCHAU TRAN, Jeff Lewis, Dave Baxter, Chad Bowden, David Irgang, James Kralik, Emerson Kasak, Matthew Johnson, Paul Rose Jr., Shannon, Dr. Charles Elbert Norton III, Edward Nycz Jr., Jessica Meuth, Caledonia, GMarkC, Chris Cheek, Bianca Tatjana Višić Ritorto, John Otway Jr, Brett Bennett, Jason 'XenoPhage' Frisvold, Scott Chisholm, Amanda Sarah, Alexandra Corrsin, Giles Fox, Rick Parker, H, Rob Steinberger, Alec Loases, David Stephenson, Anthony James Frandsen, JohnDoe, Joshua Easter, MadCatter (Cat Fleming), Kevin Potter, Bill Lisse, Michael Szewczyk, Robert Woods Tienken, Ronald L Weston, Karen Haughn, Shem Bingman, Susan Wilson, Brigitte Ziegler, Matt Soucy, Alyssa, Michelle Pelo, Richard A Shirley, PerryC, Elizabeth Kiefer, Tim, Nicolas Mandujano

III, Karen Roads, Rhel ná DecVandé, Zeb Berryman, Al Gonzalez, S. D., Jörn Flath, Rick Radzville, Aaron Loren, Justise Briones(That/Them), Genevieve Slunka, Michael DeCarlo, Kitty Crab, Jeanne L. Warner, Vi Ta, Bridget D Laurent, Jaime Bialer, Wendy Martinez, Nicholas Harezga, Mira Hunter, Cara Reasner, Lori Case, Melevorn, Rebecca Hill, Jane R., Talia Denham, Jordan Harju, Jesse Coe, Greg Levick, and Andrew Messiah.

The Golden Locket
Book 11 of the Obsidian Spindle Saga

By:
Russell Nohelty

Edited by:
Leah Lederman

Proofread by:
Katrina Roets

Cover by:
JV Arts

Formatting by:
Turbo Kitten Industries

CHAPTER 1
NIMUE

I chose to marry Hastur. It was a rash decision, made in the heat of the moment, but I had agreed to it all the same, and couldn't back out now without consigning myself to immediate torture and likely death. Now, all I could do was live with the consequences of my decision.

"Are you sure this is wise?" Cassandra asked after Hastur sent me away and I fell into her arms on the way back to my room. "Those who have resigned themselves to that fate have never lived more than a few days."

"It was absolutely not wise, but it was the only choice I had to make."

She brought me back to my room and tried to heal me, but the wounds were magically imbued to prevent such things. I had learned as much when I nursed Delilah back to health after her beating at his hands during my first days in the castle. The pain was written all over her face then, but she refused to show it, and I did my best to mimic her stoic power now. Unfortunately, I had never been good with physical pain, and Beatrice's body was not accustomed to it, either, which made it all the harder to keep how deeply I suffered written all over my face.

"I made him promise not to touch me until the wedding, in lust or in anger," I replied, willing myself from wincing. "And he swore not to touch any other for as long as I obeyed him. Weddings take time to plan, so that should buy me a few months, at least."

There was no love lost between any of the princesses that served at the King in Yellow's behest. It was a constant struggle not to fall into his crosshairs and that, more than anything, caused them to be catty and cold to each other. They would turn on each other in an instant to avoid his wrath, and that drove Cassandra to act. It was a wicked deed, but the longer I knew Hastur, the more I understood why she did it.

I hoped that my sacrifice at the dark lord's hand would bind them together against a common enemy. Now, they did not have to worry about the misery he brought upon them. I would take all their punishment for as long as I was able, and shield them from pain until my dying breath.

"He has never kept his word when it did not further his ends. He will find a way to manipulate your words against you."

Cassandra placed her hand on my lacerations. She still wore my skin, and it hung from her face, loose and unhealthy. She looked more a monster now than she did without skin, truth be told, and I had at one time hated her for taking it. However, in my short time in the castle I grew to understand her plight and now sympathized with her. She was also one of the few women in the universe who understood my own predicament, which made me trust her implicitly, even given her past transgressions.

"I have no doubt of that, Cassandra, but I have dealt

with powerful men who wished me ill all my life. I have supreme confidence that I can bend the king to my will, and not the other way around."

The muscles of her mouth twitched, but the skin did not move with them. "I appreciate your confidence, Nimue, but you have never seen one as cruel and manipulative as the King in Yellow. He is every bit the equal of any other in malice and cruelty. To think otherwise is folly."

I pushed myself to stand despite the pain. "Can you please wrap me in the gauze Bethel left on the table so that I do not bleed through my dress?"

"Of course," Cassandra replied, rising and taking the wrap from the table. "What do you plan to do?"

I raised my hands above my head. "Bring down a god, of course, before he can terrorize any others, or kill me."

Cassandra wrapped the gauze around my chest, pulling it taut so that it didn't slip. Every time she passed my wounds, it sent a shiver of pain through me.

"I'm sorry," she said. "The pain will be over soon."

"You are wrong," I replied. "I will have to withstand an untold amount before the end. That much I know for sure. I only hope I can survive long enough to find the king's weakness and take him down."

She ripped the gauze with her teeth and pressed it tightly down against my side. "If there is a weakness in the king, I do not know it, and no others have mentioned a whisper of it in my presence."

I went to my closet. "You have never spoken with all your sisters at once before, have you?"

She shook her head. "No. Sometimes I dined with Elvira, and I had tea with Delilah on occasion, but the others walled themselves off from me."

I picked out a slip and put it on, the soft cloth of it

burning my back and shoulders at even the slightest touch. "And that has worked to Has—" I remembered then that there was an enchantment in using his name, which called him forth and let him sneak in on any conversation. "—the king's advantage. Today, we eliminate that advantage."

"How?" Cassandra asked.

"Together, the six of us are more powerful than any one alone. I believe that, between us, we can find a weakness in him and exploit it." I faced her. "I still do not completely trust you, but in this place, you are the only that I can give this task. Call the princesses together. Tell them it is of utmost importance that I see them immediately."

"And if they will not come?"

In the moments after my lashing, the six of us came together in a way I didn't think possible, as a unit, and agreed to work together in an effort to kill Hastur and take his head as our trophy. Still, it was a fractious partnership, and Cassandra was right to question it. I did not have that luxury. If I didn't believe fully in our alliance, then I was condemning myself to death.

"They will come. They must. Their future queen demands it."

A black statue in the corner of the room let out a loud shriek, and in its wake, my betrothed spoke in a booming voice. "Nimue, I have need of you."

Cassandra shook with fear, and her eyes, hidden partially behind the flaps of the skin on her forehead, were wide with panic.

"It's okay, my friend," I said in a soft voice. "I have used what power I have to safeguard this room from prying ears. Call the princesses and have them meet together once I am done with him."

"And if you do not survive this encounter?"

I smirked. "Better men have tried and failed, but if the worst happens, then it falls on you to carry the torch, and make me a martyr to the cause."

"I don't know if I can do that."

I placed my hand on her loose face. "I believe in you."

"Why?" she said, softly, leaning into my hand. "I have done nothing to prove that kind of faith."

"Because I must, Cassandra. Because we all must. Killing the King in Yellow is everything for every one of us. It is all that matters."

CHAPTER 2

ARIEL

After defeating Loki, Hypnos led us back to his palace, where he secured both the god of mischief and my sister deep in the bowels of the Emerald City. When we finally emerged into the glimmering emerald gleam of the castle, he turned to me with a glint in his pink eyes.

"Thank you for your service to the Dream Realm," he said, his voice dour. "I hate to ask more of you, but there are few I trust among gods or men anymore."

"Why is that?" I asked.

"The reasons are complicated, but—in the past years, a sickness has spread among my people, one that has turned even the righteous selfish, and twisted the weak-willed into the worst kind of monster." He sighed. "As for humanity, they were created in our image, with all the ego and self-centeredness, but without an eternity to temper their tempers. They look only to the nearest moment, and never to the long-term. They cannot be trusted—save for ones like you, who do the right thing for its own sake."

I furrowed my eyebrows. "I do not know about all that,

but I have lived in the dark for too long not to move to the light now."

For almost three hundred years, I lived in the underwater castle of Ursula, queen of the sea, blind to the machinations of the surface world, unaware of the light that existed just out of my reach. Now that I had felt it, I had no interest in going back.

"Those are prescient words, and they give me pause, as what you must do now will take you into a darkness like you have never experienced."

My eyes narrowed. "You're talking about the Nightmare Realm." I knew this because when Hypnos saved me from my duplicitous sister, he told me that the right eye of Rapunzel was there, and that it was incumbent on me to find it.

"I am," he replied. "Even though my brother is dead, I have been barred from entering there. Even if I could, none would trust me enough to give direction to my quest. Unlike this place, that I control with every inch of my being, I am as ineffective in Sprig as a child cast adrift in a vast ocean."

"I understand," I said. "If you have need of Rapunzel's eye to save the Dream Realm, then I will do my duty and deliver it to you, my lord."

"I hoped you would say as much." He reached out his hand. "Then come along."

I placed my hand into his and together we vanished into the abyss. We materialized again on the top of a giant mountain, high above the plains of Oz. A range of snow-topped mountains expanded into the horizon, and a chilly bitterness whipped against my cheek.

"This is the Mountain Realm, isn't it?" I asked, breathlessly. I had spent so much time below the sea that the idea of staring down at the whole of the world was completely foreign to me. The whole range of mountains speckled the sky, but we stood above them all.

"Yes," Hypnos replied. "And this is what remains of Agrona's castle."

A horrible mouth, carved into the mountain, spewed rock that barred any from entering, though I had no idea why any would want to do so. Hypnos clapped his hands together and placed them on the edges of the caved-in entrance. I watched as time stood still and then seemed to fold back in on itself. Whatever damage befell the great keep disappeared as the rocks reformed, creating a hallway lined with paintings. A spongy tongue plumped up to carry us onward. When he was done, the collapsed mountain was completely restored. The snowy mountain top glistened like its brethren around it, shining like a beacon above them all.

Hypnos beckoned me forward. My bare feet touched the spongy tongue and the feel of the rough, course, undulating ground sent a shudder up my spine. However, I stayed behind him, clinging closer than seemed comfortable, hoping for protection from anything that waited to attack.

The hallway broke into a pristine throne room, but Hypnos ignored its many treasures, walking towards a tall, faceless wall that rose thirty feet or more into the air.

"Yes, I can feel its power here," Hypnos said when he stopped in front of the wall.

"What power?" I asked.

He turned to me. "Maybe Agrona didn't even know it when she chose this as her castle, but the veil between Urgu and the Nightmare Realm is thinner here than anywhere else. No wonder she worked so hard to keep me from this place."

He returned to examining the wall, running his fingers along its rough surface. After several minutes inspecting it, he placed his palm on a rock near the center.

"This is how I will enter the Nightmare Realm?"

He nodded. "I can almost push my fingers through to the other side myself, but it is just out of my grasp. Powerful as I am in this place, my mother set limits on what my brother and I could do." He held up the eye. "However, with this, I believe I can make a path to the other side."

My heart leapt into my chest. I had only heard stories of the monsters that came through from the Nightmare Realm, and of the great battles waged to save the Dream Realm from complete destruction. Could I hope to survive the monstrosities I would face on the other side of the portal?

"Are you sure this is a good idea?" I asked. "The last time this portal was opened, Urgu was infested with horrible monsters."

"I was not here, then," Hypnos said. "Please trust that I know what I'm doing, both in opening this portal, and choosing you as my champion."

I took a deep breath. "I will...I do...trust you I mean."

"Then let us begin."

He closed his eyes and muttered under his breath for a long time. The air whipped through the room, and then, with a thunderous boom, an enormous red portal swirled in front of me, half the size of the wall itself.

"I will keep it open as long as I can," he said. His voice was slightly strained. "But make haste. My power is great, but it is not infinite."

"How will I find the eye?" I asked, the thunder of the void forcing me to scream to be heard even as I walked closer.

"The eye craves power. Follow where it leads, and you will find the eye."

I wished that the gods would speak plainly, without riddles and double-speak, but that was not their way. This was as good as I would get. It wasn't even clear he knew what he was doing, but what was clear as I stepped through the portal was from this point I was on my own.

CHAPTER 3

ROSE

"Do you see this here?" Kadlu said, holding up a baggy of blue crystals. We had not poked our head above ground in three days, nervous that Rama and whatever cabal he hired to kill Kadlu would be on the hunt. For the most part, we stayed in the shack that acted as the goddess's safehouse from the acid rain that pounded outside and from whoever wanted her dead.

Rama didn't want me dead along with Kadlu, even if he had a funny way of showing it. If he did, I never would have agreed to go back to the Celestial Realm to save his life from whatever organism was eating his brain.

"It looks like rock salt," I replied.

Kadu examined the bag's content. "It does, doesn't it? But don't put it on your dinner. It will literally kill you if you're not infected with the Spore."

This morning she left the safehouse early in a frenzy after receiving a phone call on a line that I thought dead. The phone had been mostly eaten by the acid water that slid under the foundation and leaked into the room most of the day, leaving only the half-eaten receiver and a speaker box hanging loosely.

She didn't say a word when the call came in. She simply leapt up and dashed through the door without saying goodbye. We weren't the best of friends, but over the days of isolation we had shared stories about each other's lives. Not much at first, being wary of each other for many reasons. Her because there had been an attempt of her life moments after I sauntered into her office, and me because of all the terrible things Rama said about her.

But soon the truth came into focus, at least from Kadlu's perspective. If she was to be believed, then Rama was the evil one. Somehow, a plague, or a spore, had infected him and turned him against her, warping his brain and twisting it to a path of conquest and destruction. I found it a hard pill to swallow, especially because the cause Rama backed when I first met him was to bring down the Board and institute democratic elections in the Celestial Realm for the first time in eons.

"Then don't give it to me, you loon," I replied when she tried to hand it to me.

Of course, if he was to be trusted, then why did he try to kill me? I had gone over it a hundred times since the explosion in Kadlu's office, and nothing else made sense. Rama and I were the only two people who knew my plan, save for Chelle, and she would never turn on me.

Gods, I missed her.

"We don't have much choice in the matter. Rama trusts few, and you have won his graces."

I allowed her to place the plastic bag in my hand. "If he trusts me, then why did he try to kill me?"

"It wasn't personal," Kadlu replied, her face soft and

glowing. "He would do anything to kill me and gain what I have taken from him. Which reminds me—"

She pulled the brahmastra from the far end of the shack. It glistened in her hand. Rama had used the lance-like weapon to slay the demon king Ravana, thereby earning his place as a god.

"It's incredible that he would kill you for something so trivial."

"Not the whole weapon." She pointed to the gold inlaid in the blade. "Just this, which he can use to forge a new key to the Dark Planet and bring forth untold evil onto the world."

"Are you sure we should be giving it back to him, then?"

She bit her lip. "I am not sure about much, but without it, you will be questioned. If you bring this back with you, his excitement will overpower his common sense."

I held up the bag. "And that's when I use this?"

She nodded. "If I'm right, then this will kill the disease controlling his brain, and give him clarity for the first time in an age."

"What is it?" I peered at it more closely.

She sighed. "It's magic, old, dark, deep magic; the type which shouldn't be called without good reason, because it could disrupt the foundation of our whole universe."

I let out a small laugh. "Oh great. That's all I need, to cause the destruction of the cosmos."

"Without it, whatever has infected Rama's brain will take root even deeper, its horrible vision will grow from an impossibility to an improbability, and eventually manifest into an inevitability. We must stop it before there is no turning back."

"Okay," I replied. "You've made your point. Please, no more speeches."

Kadlu reached over and opened the bag. I jittered as she pulled a single crystal out using just her thoughts and left it hovering between us. "This is enough to destroy the spores."

I looked down at what was left. "And what about the rest?"

"He will not be the only one turned, and with any luck his memory will lead us to the others." She pointed to the bag. "The rest is for them."

"Oh great," I replied. "An army of infected gods. That's just peachy."

"Listen carefully." She concentrated on the crystal. "*Sahaq.*" The crystal jittered in the air and crumbled into fine dust. "*Rih.*"

With a flick of her fingers, the dust plumed across the room. I scooted back until I slammed against the wall. The ground was still wet with acid rain, and the burning under my hand made me scream. The sand neared my mouth, but just as it did, it stopped in midair, and then retreated into Kadlu's hands.

"That is all it takes," she said. She muttered another incantation and the sand reformed into a crystal, which she placed back into the bag. "Remember those words."

I zipped the bag. "I will."

"Then I have nothing else to show you." She handed me the brahmastra. "May the gods carry you on your journey."

"And not stop me before I can fulfill it."

She raised an eyebrow. "Well spotted. Probably not the best idea to invoke the gods right now."

"Not when they are trying to kill us."

"Not all of us." Kadlu smiled. I didn't know whether she meant not all gods were trying to kill us, or that the gods weren't trying to kill all of us, but before I could ask, she rose to her feet and opened the hatch to the tunnels underneath the city. "We must make haste. Every second we delay brings Rama's doom closer to fruition."

CHAPTER 4
BETHEL

"Let my pain be your pain," I growled at the puny sod who found himself on the wrong side of my cat-o-nine tails. I wasn't sure what he had done to deserve such torture, only that the King in Yellow demanded it, and his will must be done, else I find myself at the wrong side of his fury.

"Pleeeease!" the ugly man shouted as I lacerated his back, opening a half dozen tiny gashes.

I had no mercy to give, and none would be given to me should I fail. My master required a flagon full of suffering. I looked under the whimpering body to find that I was barely half-full of the crude needed to sustain Hastur and keep me in his graces.

"Do not beg me, cur!" I screamed. The man's back was so raw that another lash would add nothing. Instead, I exchanged my whip for a filet knife, and dug into the man's thigh. He writhed in agony, and the black bile of his suffering funneled into the flagon below.

"Sister." Cassandra stood in the doorway of the torture chamber, waving. "Might I have a word with you."

"How dare you disturb my work!" I screamed, slashing

through the air at her until she yelped, giving me the upper hand in our exchange. Cassandra always ceded her advantage to me the moment she looked into my cold, glassy black eyes.

"I'm sorry, sister, but I have need of a moment of your time, if you can spare it from your important work."

I looked back at the man, whimpering on the table while his blood drained down into the colander below. It separated his suffering from the bile and blood that seeped out with it.

"Very well," I replied, cocking my head from one side to the other. "I suppose this one has been thoroughly drained for the moment. I don't wish to kill him after all—at least, not yet."

"Thank you, mistress," the man said, whimpering.

"Don't speak, cur. I only wish not to kill you so I can use you later for the same purpose. If I keep you within an inch of your life for long enough, you might even prove some worth to me."

I stepped out into the stone hallway and slammed the iron door. The cool of the basement always refreshed me after a long torture session, and the wind whipping through the corridor nearly made me smile.

"Thank you, sister," Cassandra said, dipping her head, and then her body, in a low curtsy.

"Your pleasantries will not save you," I hissed. "Speak plainly. I have no use for flowery words."

"Yes, your grace." The fear dripped off her. It was so sweet that I would get a toothache if I drank it. "Your presence is requested by the queen."

"Future queen," I growled. "Should she live long enough to accept the crown."

I reached for the black thorn crown on my head. It was

the royal crown, bound for the queen, but until that moment, Hastur had given it to me for safekeeping, a sign of his affection. The thorns of it dug deep into my skin, but I enjoyed the pain. It heightened my emotions and kept me laser focused on the mission at hand.

"Of course, sister."

"We are not family," I spat. "You should know that better than anyone. You wear your betrayal on your skin."

She stepped backward, her loose skin rippling. I did not have to be so cruel, but I did so enjoy it. Perhaps it was better than torture, or simply that of a different nature.

"You are right, of course."

"I know I am," I answered. "It is my nature to be right. Now, about this queen you serve. Where does she request I go, and when?"

"She requests your presence in her powder room in the hour. I have already convinced Delilah, Elvira, and Lydia to attend, and now I come for you."

"Why would she need to see us all at the same time?"

Cassandra's eyes dropped and she took a step back towards me, lowering her voice. "To discuss matters of utmost importance."

Of course she meant the death of the King in Yellow, an absurd notion that had not worked in a thousand coup attempts of the past. *What made her think that she would succeed where so many had failed, even my own kin?* Still, I had no love for Hastur. He had built his harem from the death of our families, and that was the only thing that bound us together as one...loss, and hatred for the one that destroyed our lives.

"I have no love for the...for Nimue, but you can count on my attendance. Now if you will excuse me."

I spun back to the door, letting myself lose my thoughts

in the death of Hastur, and how satisfying it would be to rip the heart from his chest. I would very much like to see the look on his face as he laid on the ground, his heart in my hands as I squeezed the last breath from it.

A twitch of a smile crossed my face, though I suppressed it. Hastur's death was too much to wish for, but I supposed it couldn't hurt to go and listen. Or it could, but I would do it anyway. If nothing else, it would give me fodder to turn on the other princesses and ingratiate myself more as Hastur's favorite. That was how I survived until now, and if what it took to keep surviving was to turn on them, I would throw them all to the wolves without a second thought.

CHAPTER 5

RED

After Zeus's death at my hand, everything changed. I was freed from my solitary confinement in the Crystal Keep and took an esteemed position at Rama's side. Athena was stripped of her rank and forced into a private cell for dissidents until it could be determined whether or not she would be a problem for the new order of things.

Zeus had been the figure the rest of the Board rotated around. Rama, Brahma, Ukko, and Svarog hate him, while Osiris and Tengri loved him. Either way, without him at the center of their world, everything was fracturing.

"Will you come with me?" Rama asked after a particularly grueling meeting with what remained of the Board. He slumped against my shoulder as I led him to Zeus's old office. Since the god's death—or murder depending on how you saw it—Rama had taken temporary control of Zeus's seat, but was prevented from voting on any matters of import until a proper replacement could be found.

"Of course," I replied, bearing his whole weight. Rama held a terrible secret from the Board. Zeus had stripped out the piece of divining in him, turning him from a god back into a human. Ceaseless activity and movement had never bothered Rama before, but without the strength of a god or the conditioning of an athlete, it took its toll on him.

"I'll get you some water." I went to a small refrigerator I'd brought in under the guise that I needed to keep food nearby to maintain my strength. I didn't, of course, but I couldn't rightly say the real reason was because Rama was a human.

"Thank you," he replied weakly after taking a sip. "I will never get used to this cursed human body."

"I didn't find it so bad when I had mine."

"And how many eons ago was that?" he said, rolling his head to me.

"A fair few, I admit. Maybe we can—"

The door flung open, and a massive older gentleman walked in wearing a cape made of thick hair and hide. An eyepatch covered his right eye, and a crow perched on each of his shoulders.

"I am sorry to hear about your recent troubles, old friend," he said, walking with a confident swagger.

Rama nodded, shuffling over with what remained of his strength. "It is good to see you, my dear friend Odin. I hope all is well."

Odin pulled him tightly for a hug. "You have grown weak, Rama. I hope nothing is wrong with your constitution after taking your place on the Board."

"Nothing a glass of mead and a good wench cannot fix."

Odin let Rama go. He picked up the water, whose glass looked tiny in his great paw, and sniffed it. "Yet, you drink this tasteless mixture." He cocked his head at me. "And is this your wench? Not much to her."

"Excuse me, sir, but I am no wench," I said with as

much authority as I could muster. "I am personal guard to Rama."

Without a word, and in a motion too quick for my eye to catch, Odin reached into his belt and pulled out a jagged, serrated knife and held it up to Rama's throat. "Not doing a very good job, girly. That's why you don't send a human to do a god's job." He smiled and placed the dagger away without breaking eye contact with me. "Which is the purpose of my visit."

Rama sat down behind the desk with a groan. "And what purpose is that?"

Odin tapped his finger on his chin and paced idly. "It's just...I know about your little predicament."

Rama gave Odin a blank look. "And what, pray tell, is that?"

"That you are a human."

"Preposterous."

Odin, who had stopped walking momentarily while speaking to Rama, now resumed his pacing. "No, it's not. I took your friend, the gorgon one, and I hurt every little snapping snake on her otherwise pretty little head—her whole body actually. And unless I'm very wrong, I believe that breaks your bond with her sweet, little, blonde girlfriend."

Chelle. He was talking about her and Rose. I should have leapt over the table and taken him out, but instead I simply raised my golden dagger into the air. "Watch what you say. I killed two gods with this, and I have no qualms in slitting the throat of a third."

"Ha!" Odin spat without so much as a smile. "I am not as blinded by power as Zeus, nor as weak as Epiales, so please save your fantasies for Urgu."

I couldn't hold it another second. I lunged forward and

would have sliced Odin in half if Rama did not step between us.

"You can't let him push you around, Rama!" I shouted.

He held up his hand. "It's okay, Gabrielle. Odin and I have much to discuss. After all, we are old friends, with old grudges. This could take a while. Why don't you go, and I will call you when I have need of you."

"You can't possibly think that I would—"

"I am still on the Board, and thus you work for me!" Rama snapped. "I am trying to be polite, but go, or I will have you taken, unless you think I am as weak as Odin does. If that is the case, I will show you both just how wrong you are."

I bit my lip and glared at him. "If that is your wish, then I will see it granted."

I was used to being kicked out of important meetings, but somehow the sting of it never faded. Still, I went, and when I closed the door on them, I swore I heard laughter peal through the room. Powerful men, it seemed, were the same, no matter what side of the aisle they fought.

CHAPTER 6

ROSE

It took us a full day to trek up the mountain to find the Obsidian Spindle on her planet. Kadlu could have brought me in an instant, but she contended that if Rama saw me unruffled by the journey, he would know something was wrong. Besides, we had to make sure she wasn't being followed, and that meant an arduous trek.

At least it didn't rain until we were above the cloud cover, and the mist that plumed from it barely burned my skin. When we reached the top of the cliff, I gazed upon the sight that had once filled me with both awe and dread. The Obsidian Spindle looked the same on every planet, except the Celestial Realm, where the portals originated. A tall, black tower rose high in the air, like the Eye of Sauron, but somehow more ominous. Its surface glistened, untarnished by weather and use.

"This way." Kadlu was winded but in high spirits, and why shouldn't she be? If she was to be believed, and I certainly believed her, then she had been planning to save Rama for more than a century.

She stuck Rama's brahmastra into the earth and moved

to the Spindle. Every lock was a little different, depending on the god who had built and maintained it. This one was a puzzle box, with pieces of rock needing to be moved in specific ways to open it up. She worked for several minutes, the rocks clicking together every few seconds, until finally the stone receded into the wall, revealing a white light within.

"Thank you," I said.

"If you can save my love, then I will be the one thanking you." Kadlu slid the brahmastra's blade across her hand and sucked in her breath as it drew blood. When the blade was sufficiently coated, she placed the staff in my hand. "Tell him it was a bitter fight, but you won in the end."

I frowned. "Then you should hit me."

"I don't want to do that," she said. "I might not like you, but I have grown fond of you."

"If it was a bitter fight, then I need the wounds to prove it."

She seemed to consider this for a moment, and then, faster than I could track, she punched me once on either side of my face, and again in the stomach. I dropped to the ground, coughing blood.

"Good enough?" she asked. "I could go on."

"Scorch marks," I said, turning my side to her. "Burn my clothes and rip the sleeve. Leave a piece of nail if you can."

"I don't think this is fair. You don't even get to hit me."

I rose to my feet, using the hilt of the brahmastra to support my shaky body. "You're right. If it was bloody, then I need to get a hit on you, too."

Kadlu nodded. "I'm ready."

I moved out from behind the weapon and clocked her across the cheek. She barely moved, and my knuckles crumpled under the pressure. I wasn't much for fighting, at least not with my fists. "Ow."

"Not so easy to fight a god." She grinned. "My turn."

I squeezed my eyes shut. She muttered an incantation, and my left side went up in flames. I dropped to the ground, screaming, and rolled out the burn, but the side of my shirt was singed, and my body was red and black with deep burns.

"This really sucks," I said, my breath ragged. "Now, the sleeve."

"Are you sure this isn't enough?" Kadlu asked. "You are damaged already."

I held my shoulder out to her. "Just do it."

She ripped my sleeve violently, her nails digging into my arm and leaving streaks of blood as she pulled away. I was bloody, burned, and inches from unconsciousness, but I was alive, which meant I still had a chance to end all of this terribleness.

"Well, this isn't the way I wanted to say goodbye," Kadlu said, half laughing. "You've been a better friend to me than most, which says more than I care to admit about my life, considering you came here to steal from me, and your presence nearly got me killed."

"Some of the best friendships are based upon theft," I said with a bloody smile.

"You will tell him that I love him, if you can bring him back to normal, won't you?" Kadlu asked quietly.

I nodded. "He will know how you feel should I succeed in saving him."

She moved closer and touched her forehead to mine. "I wish I could give you my blessing, but we both know that would be a dead giveaway." She reached into her pocket and pulled out a small blue gem. "This will prevent anyone from reading your mind, no matter how powerful they are."

"I can't take this. He'll know—"

"No, he won't." Kadlu shook her head as she pressed the gem into my head, behind my left ear. It stung briefly and then it was over. "He won't even know it's there."

I rubbed my finger against the back of my ear and felt the smoothness of my skin. She was right. I couldn't feel anything. "Thank you."

I pressed my forehead to hers again and took one last look back at her face, so full of hope and love, before stepping through the portal back to the Celestial Realm.

CHAPTER 7
NIMUE

Hastur's quarters were dark, ominous, and filled with traps. The last time I visited him, glowing orbs of light rained down upon me and burned my skin. No matter how beautiful the surroundings, everything in his domain was designed to harm.

Stepping through the doorway into his room, I heard the distinct sounds of growling and deep breathing coming from the darkness. Unnatural creatures lurked there, but they were not what worried me most. A field of red orchids filled the room, glowing a neon hue.

The hairs on my neck bristled at the horrors they could unleash with their plumes. I held my breath as I passed, expecting them to lash out at me, but they sat dormant. They had a pleasant aroma, like the ones I loved back on Earth. I had once adored flowers, before Urgu, and the anosmia that came with being a spirit in the Dream Realm. When I returned to Earth, I had every intention of tending a garden, but every orchid I bought died on the vine. Fickle flowers they were, and I did not have the temperament to keep them alive.

Keeping things alive was not a skill of mine, it turned out, and yet I was expected to save the lives of everyone on the Dark Planet, all while keeping myself alive long enough to see my vengeance carried out. I was quite adept at keeping myself alive, however. If it was a fight between Hastur's will and mine, I would bet on myself every time.

"Ah, my queen!" Hastur's voice boomed against the walls. He stepped into the light. Gone was the long, yellow robe, replaced by a sheer yellow gown with a thin silk hood. They gave no definition to his body, which seemed to hang in space like an amorphous sack of leaves taken shape as a man. "Many glad tidings to you."

"Such a pleasant greeting, my king."

He threw his arms into the air. "And why should I not be pleased? We are to be married, and then you will be mine for all time, as you have promised."

He tried to touch me, and I cringed. "And as you promised, you will not touch me until the wedding night, or any other."

"Yes, yes. I remember our accords, which is why I have wonderful news."

I stepped sideways, away from him. "And what is that, my king?"

"I have found an officiant, and we will be married at the turn of the night, in two days' time."

I raised my eyebrows, nonchalant. "Two days? That is not enough time to plan a wedding. What of the guests?"

"They will come to my palace when they are called, from every corner of the realm, or they will be punished severely."

I held out my hands. "No, my king. We need more time. I thought a year or longer to do this properly."

"Do you not want to be married to me, my dear?"

No, absolutely not. "That's not it at all. I just want it to be perfect." I gave him the biggest, fakest smile I could muster. "After all, a girl only gets married once, right?"

Hastur rubbed his chin solemnly. "You would like a year-long engagement, and I would like to be married in two days' time. So, let us compromise, and be married in two days' time."

"That is not much of a compromise, my king. That is me acquiescing to your demands."

He charged forward. "And what is marriage, but the woman succumbing to the man's wishes?"

I stared into his orange eyes. They swirled like nebulas. "That is not much of a marriage at all. It is more of an enslavement."

"Yes, now you understand. Oh, perhaps you will not die on our wedding night as so many have speculated." He cocked his head. "Perhaps you might even prove to be my equal yet."

I am more than your equal. "I hope our union lasts many happy years."

He clapped his hands together. "Happiness is not something I offer often, or freely. I have many plans for you, though. Would you like a taste?"

My smile was coy this time. "I would rather be surprised. Now, was there something you needed from me, my liege?"

"To tell you the news, and to ask what you thought of these flowers for the reception. They are a mutation on the orchids I know you love." He gestured to the flowers I'd passed. "Carnivorous, naturally, but you should be able to keep them alive with blood."

"How so?" I asked. "They gave me no trouble."

Hastur reached for one of them and placed his finger

next to the stamen. "If you get too close, then it will—" He pulled back his finger just as the petals latched tightly.

I smiled at him again, forcing my bitterness into some semblance of excitement. "I very much like them, though I will advise the guests not to touch them."

"Why on Earth would you do something like that? Seeing the look of surprise on their faces as they lose a limb is half the fun." His grin was unsettling. "I have asked the staff to prepare the queen's suite for you. It will serve you well in the time leading up to the ceremony.

"Thank you, my king." I moved carefully to avoid even brushing against the mutant orchids. "If there is nothing else, then I have much to do to prepare for the wedding."

"Have you chosen your bridesmaids yet?" he asked.

"I thought the other princesses would do a fine job. They know this land better than anyone, and this castle as well as your most loyal attendants."

He lifted his eyes to the ceiling. "If you can get them to agree on anything you would be the first."

I have already convinced them to kill you before the wedding. "I have spoken to them and find them charming. Lovely, even."

"That is the first time I have ever heard anyone say that. Perhaps you will make a fine queen after all."

I bowed. "I only hope to do you proud, my king."

And kill you, of course.

CHAPTER 8
ARIEL

A blast of cold air met me when I stepped into the Nightmare Realm...though it was not as dark as I expected. Every surface was covered in luminescent plants and trees, pulsating with orange, green, blue, and violet light. Small creatures skittered away from me through the grass.

"You don't have to be scared of me," I called out. "I'm not going to hurt you."

The truth was, I was much more afraid of anything in the Nightmare Realm than they could ever be of me. Still, there was a life to this place, a beauty I didn't expect, and the sight of it took me aback.

A bush rustled, and I raised my arms to confront whatever came for me. From the darkness hopped a bunny... except that it was made wrong. The ears were long, thin, and crooked. Hollow black, inky darkness sat where its eyes should have, and instead of squared teeth it had razor-sharp fangs.

"I have no quarrel with you, rabbit," I said in as stern a voice as I could muster. I thought for a moment of returning to the safety of the Dream Realm, but how could I look Hypnos in the eye if I could not last a single minute in the Nightmare Realm? He was counting on me, and I needed to deliver for him, and for all of Urgu. Without me, where would he turn?

The rabbit hopped closer, as if looking to intercept me. Rabbits generally ran away from conflict, but this one was like none I had ever known.

"I'm serious, rabbit," I said, louder this time. I balled up my fists. "I know magic, and I am not afraid to use it."

"Afraid to use it?" the rabbit whispered.

Out of its shadow strode a being taller than it was wide by at least double, towering like a tree, with legs so thin I was surprised that it could move without toppling over. It held a long mace in its hand and wore a skull for a face.

My stomach turned over twice, until I was knotted and twisted in such a way that I collapsed into myself.

"I thought you knew magic," the rabbit said. "I thought you were serious."

"*Augue!*" I shouted, holding out my hands. Nothing happened. "*Augue!*"

I tried again, and again, but something was preventing my magic from working. Then I remembered that Hypnos said his magic didn't work in Sprig, which must have meant that anything I received from his blessing didn't work either.

"Dream magic," the rabbit lurched forward. "Cute."

There was only one spell I knew how to cast outside of the blessing, and I screamed it as loud as I could. "*Lux!*"

From my hand a huge ball of light grew and shone through the valley. The being and its rabbit shrieked out, and I turned back to the portal. My salvation. I needed more power to face the Nightmare Realm; I was ill prepared for the journey. I hadn't taken into account all the pitfalls, or how every single inch in Sprig was meant to turn against you at a moment's notice.

My legs churned, racing back to the portal. I was right on top of it...and that was the same moment it closed upon me. My stomach dropped to my feet. Hypnos promised to keep the portal open as long as he could, and I had only been through it for a few moments. What could have possibly caused such an issue that he saw fit to close the portal? How would I get home now?

More importantly, I thought of the monsters now bearing down on me, how would I stay alive until I could find a way back home?

CHAPTER 9

RED

It stung to be forced out of Rama's meeting with Odin, but I had better things to do than be a glorified bodyguard anyway. While we waited for Rose to bring back the brahmastra, I needed to find the key master, the only person in the universe who could make a new key to the Dark Planet, apparently. That's where we would find Rapunzel—and if we found her, we'd find Nimue. I would finally have my vengeance and be sure she would never bring her wrath on anyone else.

Rama had given me the name of a minor deity living on a nearly dead world who claimed to be an apprentice of the key master several centuries ago. We were set to travel to the planet together before the unpleasantness with Zeus and the Board, and now he was too feeble to join me on any excursion out of the Celestial Realm. I was a solitary creature, so I didn't mind doing it on my own. Perhaps I even preferred it that way.

I made my way across the Celestial Realm to the portal terminal. The lines were long, as they always were. Gods loved coming home, but the only thing they loved more was leaving again. Many of the gods maintained several worlds, and some took their jobs seriously. Of course, it was just as likely to find one who treated the worlds they managed like a vacation, content to suck the marrow from a planet for their own gain.

"Where ya headed?" a centaur asked as I queued up in the line next to them. There were six teleporters in total, and they had to be calibrated to a new planet with each use, but the porters who worked the portals were relatively quick about it. All of the gods were grumbling, though. When you were used to the immediacy of godhood, any delay felt like an eternity.

I would have preferred to stand in silence, but it was rude to do so, unfortunately, so I gave the centaur a smile. He wore a tie and a sports jacket, and his mane was quaffed to perfection.

"Just running an errand for my boss," I replied. "Hope it doesn't take long."

"They always take longer than they should, am I right?" He smiled at me, and his perfect teeth shone brightly.

"They always do," I said. "Where are you going?"

He sighed. "My boss got in a speck of trouble with a greater deity, so I have to go try and smooth things over before it leads to war between—well, you know how gods are. Even the smallest slight can become a world-ending phenomenon."

I chuckled. "You are not wrong, but should you be saying things like that?"

He smiled even brighter. "Are you kidding? Do you think the gods care about what we say? They aren't even paying attention."

I looked around to see the gods staring forward, bored, as if the rest of us didn't exist. We could have screamed bloody murder and they would have barely noticed, except that we got blood on their shoes.

"I guess that's one benefit of not being one."

He rolled his eyes. "There are so many benefits to not being a god I'm not even sure I can list them all."

"I heartily agree with you. What is your name, friend?"

"This is really embarrassing, but my boss calls me Horse, and the name stuck."

"Yes, that is embarrassing," I replied. "I'm Gabrielle, but people call me Red."

"Hail and hearty to you." He reached into his pocket and pulled out a business card. "If you ever need my services, you can find me there."

The card was covered with moons and stars. He wasn't lying that his name was Horse, but it wasn't the most demeaning thing I had heard. I was once rescued by an apsara that didn't even have a name—she died without one.

"What god do you work for?"

"Erebus, god of darkness...and drama."

"Ah yes," I replied. "I met his ex-wife, Nox."

"Is she as terrible as her husband?"

"I don't know how bad he is, but she is a drama queen." I sighed. I didn't feel like going through the whole of my story with a stranger I just met. "But she's okay, in her way."

His brow furrowed. "Is something wrong with Nox? My benefactor would want to know something like that."

I opened my mouth to answer but heard a commotion. The whole of the lines crowded around something that had just been spat from the portal. Exclamations of "my word" and "good heavens" filled the station as I squeezed through the front. When I saw what had tumbled from the portal, I covered my mouth.

There, crumbled on the ground, beaten and bruised, barely clinging to consciousness or the bloody staff in her hand, was Rose.

She looked up at me with a smile that showed her bloody teeth. "Hi, Red. I think I need your help."

CHAPTER 10

BETHEL

I should have told Hastur immediately what the other princesses were planning. Not doing so made me complicit. I hadn't said yes when Nimue said we had to kill the King in Yellow, but neither did I turn her over to him for her treachery. To him, those were equally treasonous offenses. Any slight, no matter how small, was retaliated against with extreme prejudice.

If I wanted to remain on his good side, I needed to infiltrate their ranks and learn more about their duplicity. Only then could I bring my findings to Hastur, reveal my loyalty to him, and be absolved of my crimes.

It was for that reason and that reason alone that I left the dungeon and followed the stairs up to the living area. Nimue had been moved from her room nearest the doorway to one befitting her new station. It took three turns to find it, and only if you knew where you were going. Otherwise, you would be lost in the labyrinth.

The queen's chambers were the only one with ivory doors, but they still depicted the same monstrous tortures of all the others, carved deep into the grain in the same way I carved myself into those who suffered at my boot. Noises came from inside the room, and when I went to the door it opened for me.

Cassandra had become a favorite of Nimue since she arrived at the castle. I didn't know why, as it was her treason that led to the future queen being skinned alive. It was Nimue's skin that Cassandra wore, ill-fitting and horrific. It tickled me to watch them both laid low, bearing their failed plot against Hastur all over them, especially since they were conspiring again, and believed that this time would be successful. Delusion was a powerful drug.

"You have arrived," Cassandra said. "We have been waiting for you."

I entered the room and saw my sisters, the other princesses marred by Hastur into hideous monsters. Elvira, pure white with red eyes and six horns protruding from the top of her head. Delilah with haunted forest paints on the cracks in her skin, and Lydia, a universe contained upon herself, with a galaxy spinning where her head should be. Finally, Nimue. The usurper; skinless, yet formidable. There was a strength about her that gave me pause.

"I am glad you have arrived," Nimue said, standing from her leather chair in the center of them all. "I was afraid we would have to collect you some other way."

"You could have tried," I replied, cocking my head slightly. "But I believe you will find it harder to force me to do anything than it would be to retrieve your skin."

The faces of my princess brethren were stoic at my words. They had truly felt horrors, and my words were nothing to them.

"I have dealt with worse than you in my time," Nimue

replied. "However, I do appreciate your strong-willed spirit."

"What are we doing here?" Lydia asked. She had no lips, but her words bore into my brain all the same. "The king is sure to suspect us."

"No," Nimue said. "I have named you all my bridesmaids, and he has staked the wedding in two days' time, which means we will have reason to see much of each other until then."

"Two days?" Elvira said. "That is not enough time."

"If it is enough to plan a wedding, it is long enough to plan an assassination," Nimue said, matter of fact in a way that I almost admired.

"He will kill you before then," Delilah added.

Nimue shook her head. "He has agreed not to touch any who work or live in the castle until the wedding, though I fear he plans to break me on our wedding night."

"Kill you," I said. "He will kill you on your wedding night, most assuredly."

Nimue's eyes blazed as they focused on me. "Then we must kill him first."

"Hundreds of others have tried, including you if I'm not mistaken, and every time it has failed. What makes you think you are so special as to do what they didn't?"

"Easy," Nimue replied. "Because this time we won't betray each other." There was a gasp around the room. "Yes, I know the reason why these attempts have failed. Just like when Cassandra betrayed me, Hast—the king—relies on you to tell him of the schemes set up against him. If none of us break, then he will never be the wiser."

"He is wiser than you could ever imagine," I hissed.

"No!" Cassandra shouted. "He is only as wise as we allow him to be. Nimue is right. We are the key to his successful rule, so if we keep our mouths sealed, then we can do this."

"And what is to stop one of us from breaking?" Elvira asked.

"Solidarity, and the knowledge that the only way he dies is if we work together."

Delilah spoke next. "What if one of us doesn't want him dead?"

"I have thought of that," Nimue said. "And if you can look at yourself and say that you would save the man who slayed your families, who turned you into what you are now, and who forces you to exact cruelty most foul, is—if he is who you want to throw your support behind, then I cannot stop you. I will not stop you. I would rather die fighting to save this kingdom from a tyrant than—"

"And who would take his place? What tyrant would come to rule instead of him? You?" I stepped closer, until my face nearly touched hers. "Because there is always another tyrant."

"Not if we lead...together."

Another gasp in the room. I narrowed my eyes. "Are you truly saying that the power of the crown should be shared among each of us?"

Nimue strode away from me and walked through the gathered princesses. "I am. Equal power to do equal good. That is what I propose, what I offer should the yellow king die at my hand."

"That sounds like the kind of thing a tyrant proposes before they stab us in the back," Lydia said.

Nimue pulled a knife from a hidden sheath on her calf and held out her hand. "I will make a blood oath with you all, if you would make one with me. One for all, and all for one."

The eyes shifted around the room. Then, Cassandra spoke up. "I will make that pact with you."

"We have one!" Nimue shouted. "Who will join me, and who wants to live in tyranny for the rest of their lives?"

Elvira stood next, followed by Lydia. Delilah turned to me, as if trying to read my thoughts, and then she stood, too. All of them held out their hands to me.

"What do you say?" Nimue asked. "We can't be all for one, if one of us denies the rest. I won't take up arms against any of you, but I will ask you to join us."

Join them? In an alliance? My head spun trying to imagine what would happen if the King in Yellow died, if I no longer had to bend a knee to him. Was such a world even possible? Was it worth risking it for the simple possibility of freedom, true freedom, like I hadn't felt in longer than I could remember?

These were the strongest women I knew. No, the strongest people. Together, they represented the most powerful alliance in the history of the king's reign, but if he found out what we were planning to do...it would be a terrible vengeance. He would take our powers, lay us low, and grind us into the ground. He wouldn't kill us, that would be too kind. He would see us suffer until we were inches from death, and then pull us back to do it again and again.

I had watched him do it. I had invoked his wrath myself. It was a terrible retribution.

"You are his pet," Elvira said to me. "Which is why we need you most of all. He will never suspect you, and you can feed him pleasant falsehoods until it is too late."

"Do you truly think me a pet?" I asked, bristling.

"I do, because it is the truth," Elvira said with a calm, even voice.

"We all are his pets," Delilah said. "That's why we're all doing this in the first place. We deserve better."

Better? It had been long since I even imagined what that might be. Was it truly possible, or was this just a false hope? And if it was simply a false hope, was it not worth it to feel that again for one more moment in my life? Hope is a powerful drug, perhaps the most powerful delusion in the world.

Finally, I said, "I planned to betray you to him."

"I know that," Nimue said, watching me. "I hope you don't, though."

"Do you truly believe you can beat him?"

The muscles in her jaw clenched. "With everything I have. And if somehow we fail, then I will be proud that we tried, but I do not believe we will fail. Not if we are all in this together."

"In that case," I said, holding out my hand, "I will join you."

I wasn't surprised at the words I said. I had always intended to do what I must to betray them, even if it meant joining their alliance. What surprised me was that somewhere deep in a forgotten part of my soul, I believed the words. I hadn't believed in anything in so long, but now, suddenly, I had a hope that I thought long vanished, and something else underneath it. Something I never thought I would feel again.

Happiness.

Just a glint of it, but it was there, and if I could feel that jolt again, then Nimue was right. It would all be worth it, even if we failed. She cut her hand, and blood dripped onto the table. In turn, we each mixed our blood with hers, and when it was done, she muttered a spell that turned the blood a glowing blue before it returned into our bodies and the cuts healed.

"It is done," Nimue said. "Now, if any of us betray the others to the King in Yellow, we will know it and take action against them."

CHAPTER II
RED

"Maricel!" I shouted as I dragged Rose into Rama's house. She had fallen unconscious on our walk back to the mansion. "I need your help!"

Feet skittered across the hall until Rama's servant came around the corner of the library wearing a red sari. "What happened? Did you get attacked?"

"I don't know. I found her like this at the portal station."

She slipped her arm under Rose's shoulders to help bear the weight. "Let's get her up to bed."

Rama's mansion was enormous, with dozens of rooms on the first floor alone. Luckily, Rose was a waifish thing that didn't take much effort to drag forward, especially with two people. Still, even as a small person, lugging dead weight across the Celestial Realm took a toll, and by the time we threw her in bed, my back was crying out for relief.

"Thank you," I said, trying to catch my breath.

"I'll get her some water and call for a healer."

Maricel bounded out of the room and down the stairs and once she had gone, I turned my attention to Rose. I brushed away the hair matted to her bruised face, and she groaned and opened her eyes.

"Gabrielle?" She smiled at me. "Is this a dream?"

I shook my head. "No, sweetheart. You're safe now. What happened to you?"

"The brahmastra?" she asked with a sudden panic drawn on her face. "Is it okay?"

I pointed across the room, where I had placed the weapon. "It's fine. You did it, Rose. You really did it."

She winced as she shifted herself higher onto the pillows. "And Chelle?"

I bit my lip. "She was captured by Odin. I couldn't hear much after Rama kicked me out of the board room, but—"

"Wait," Rose said, leaning forward. The sheets were crumpled in her hands. "Rama was in the boardroom? Does that mean we won?"

"Not...yet," I replied. "Zeus is dead, and we hold a tenuous control, but we need Odin to secure that control."

"And he has Chelle?"

"As far as I know, yes."

"We have to get her. Now." Rose swung her legs to the floor, but her knees buckled as soon as she stood up.

"You can barely stand, let alone fight. We have called a healer, and once you are fixed up, then we'll get her back, together. We'll meet with Rama and figure this out."

There was a wild, frenetic energy in Rose's eyes as she pulled me close. "You can't trust him, Red. You can't." She gritted her teeth. "Rama's not who you think he is."

The door opened and Maricel walked into the room with a tray of food. Behind her, a short, thin man wearing a purple suit. "I've brought my friend Aziz to tend to your friend's wounds."

Rose reached into her pocket and pulled something out, stuffing it into my hand. "Hold this for me."

"What is it?"

"It's everything, Red. Whatever you do, don't tell Rama about it. Promise me."

"I promise," I said with a nod to her. "I will not betray you on this."

She pulled me close into a whisper. "See that you don't, or it could be the end of everything."

Aziz hesitated at the end of the bed. "I am afraid I will need privacy to work on your friend's wounds. I hope you understand."

I wasn't sure I did, but I was so confused by what Rose had just told me, and the ferocity of her claims, that I had no other recourse except to nod. "Of course."

"Come," Maricel said, placing the food tray on the bedside table. "Let's give them the room."

I followed Maricel and closed the door on our way out. From the other side I heard screams of pain and turned back to help, but Maricel stopped me.

"What is he doing to her?" I asked.

"Healing her."

"It sounds like he's torturing her."

"Often, healing comes from pain."

"I've known a lot of healers in my time, and none of them caused that amount of pain when they healed someone."

"Then maybe you didn't know very good healers." She grabbed my shoulder compassionately but forcefully. "Now, let's get you some tea and calm your nerves."

She said it with a gentle tone, but I knew it wasn't a question. "Okay."

I let Maricel get a few steps ahead of me on the stairs

and then I opened my palm. Rose had handed me a small plastic bag filled with blue crystal. I stuffed it back in my pocket and headed down the stairs. When we reached the bottom, Rama was there.

I looked at him, searching, trying to ascertain what Rose meant about him not being who he seemed. As far as I knew, he was a freedom fighter who cared about truth and justice, but Rose was my best friend, and she had never steered me wrong before.

"Something wrong?" he asked.

I shook my head. "Of course not. I'm just a little bitter you kicked me out today."

"Understandable, but some gods do not take kindly to humans, and Odin is old school in that way. My apologies."

"It's okay. I was just about to have some tea. Would you like to join me?"

Rama smiled. "That sounds lovely. We have a lot to discuss."

CHAPTER 12
NIMUE

I kept my hands tented in front of me as Delilah, Elvira, and finally Lydia all left the room. Cassandra, Bethel, and I remained.

"Can I talk to you frankly for a moment, Bethel?" I asked her when she moved to the door as well.

"Didn't you just?"

"I meant alone," I said, giving Cassandra a meaningful look. She closed the door on her way out.

Bethel watched her pass, staring at the door as the lock clicked, and then turned back to me. "I suppose that would be okay, considering we are alone now."

She sat on an uncomfortable pink couch that I hated. The bright décor clashed with everything else in the castle. Its gaudiness burrowed under my skin and infuriated me.

"I asked the other princesses each who they thought was the most likely to betray our mission, and they all, to a person, said you. Why do you think that is?"

Bethel sneered, but the dead holes that bled black ichor into the rest of her body didn't belie any emotion. "Jealousy, I suppose."

I pointed to her crown. "They also told me that you wear the queen's crown on your head, a sign that you are the king's favorite."

"It is not my fault that I fall into his graces, my queen."

I held up my hand. "You do not have to placate me. I know you have seen your share of potential usurpers go through this castle in your time. You have likely helped take them down yourself—by yourself, if the rumors are to be believed. Cassandra is sure that you are the reason her coup was revealed."

Bethel looked at the ceiling. "Is this going somewhere?"

"When you leave this room, the king will call you, and you will have the chance to turn on us, as you have so many times."

"And you would like me not to do so. Is that it?"

"No—well, yes, but what I ask is something much simpler. If you reveal my crimes, reveal only them, and leave our sisters out of it."

"And how would I keep them out of it, given the topic of our meeting?"

"Easy. Tell him that I kept you after the others and asked if you would help me. You refused. Tell him that you assume I offered the others the same deal."

"And did you, in this fantasy of yours?"

"No," I replied. "I spoke to you first, and then had meetings all day which would take me away from the others. This is true. I have appointments with caterers, wedding planners, and tailors. I won't have a chance to meet with you all until late this evening, which gives you enough time to implicate me and have me killed."

"And what if I simply want to watch it all burn?" Bethel asked. "I could implicate all of you. That would be easier for me, wouldn't it?"

"I'm not sure." I shrugged. "I don't know you from Eve. I would like to, but I know that is up to you, and that you have been hurt before." I stood. "I cannot convince you to do anything you are not interested in doing, but you have a great role to play in all of this, having weaseled your way into the king's confidence, and can be a great asset. But if you choose to deny us, then please, if you have any love for me, or any of us, let me take the blame for it all."

Bethel stood. "If I let them live, they will plot again."

"Maybe, but I think it will take a while for them to find another like me in a place like this, so your king will be safe for a long time if you deny me. Besides, you will always know our treachery, and if you see them fall out of line, then you can step in."

She sat quietly, studying her hand where we'd all mixed our blood in the oath we made just moments before. "Won't you know whether I betray you or not?"

I smiled. "I don't know a spell like that. What I did was give false hope to you all in hope it would bond us together."

"You started our whole relationship on a lie."

"But I told you the truth, and I will tell them all at the right moment, but our alliance is tenuous at best, and they need all the false confidence they can get, before the end."

"You are cunning," Bethel said, leaning back as if to take me in again, giving me an appraising look. "I'm not sure I've met one like you yet."

"I will take that as a compliment. Within the hour you will have to make your choice." I walked to the door. "I have obligations, but please stay here as long as you need to consider your options. Just know I will not think less of you no matter what you choose."

"Because you could not think less of me."

I shook my head. "No, because you are not responsible for your actions. We all have to survive in any way we can. This king is mean, petty, and cruel. If you stand with us, you stand with freedom, and set yourself out to be found out. When you deal with men like him, it is never a good idea to draw attention to yourself, for better or worse. I love you the same either way."

I left the room but before I did, I swore I saw a single tear fall down Bethel's alabaster face.

CHAPTER 13
ARIEL

I ran from the fields into the dark, foreboding woods as the mutilated bunny and its oblong handler chased after me. When they came within range, I shot out another blinding light, but I wasn't much of a witch. My magical energy drained after only a couple of spells. I was exhausted. It was as if the blessing I had received was a curse in this place; it weighed me down.

Something rustled in the trees, and I whipped around to see what horror waited for me. A man with shaggy hair and a messy beard pointed a bow and arrow at me.

"Are you what caused all that commotion?" he asked, his voice more of a growl than anything.

"I mean you no harm," I replied.

"That's not what I asked. Did you cause all that light or what?" he asked. "Answer me quick or I'll put an arrow in your throat and dust you right now."

I feared telling him the truth but managed, "Yes, it was me."

"Where'd you learn that?" He relaxed his bow. "I

haven't seen that kind of magic around here, and I've been here a long time."

"Do you not have magic in the Nightmare Realm?"

He frowned. "We do, but it's twisted and...wrong. What I saw was pure light. That kind of thing is hard to find in Sprig. Even those that can conjure it are too afraid of upsetting the Shadow King."

"Shadow King?"

He nodded. "He runs this place, now that Epiales and Etsop are gone, and he claims complete control of the light."

"Odd, given the name."

"Shadows only dance in the light." The man sniffed. "You smell different than any I have met before in this place."

"Is that a bad thing?"

"Not a good or bad thing"—he raised his bow— "but now I know you're not from around here. So, answer my question. Where are you from?"

"Last time somebody found out where I was from, they started hunting me, which is why I ended up in these woods at all."

"I could kill you now, stranger. I'm not good with fancy words, but I am good with a bow."

I sighed. "I come from the Dream Realm, with the blessing of Hypnos, to find something very dear to him."

His eyes turned fiery. "Don't you lie to me."

"I'm not lying," I said. "I could bring you to the portal we used if it was still there, but it vanished after I arrived, so you are either going to have to trust me or put an arrow in my throat." Twigs snapped behind me. "But think quick, because we are about to have company."

"I see no lies in you. You are filled with the same fear all have in this place." The man exhaled sharply and dropped his bow to his side once more. "Come on then."

"Are we going somewhere?"

"I know these woods better than anyone, and certainly better than some nightmare creatures conjured from the Shadow King's warped mind. If you are what you say, then I have no quarrel with you, but we need to move now."

The words had no sooner left his mouth when the misshapen creature pushed through the trees and into the clearing. The rabbit followed, leaping towards me. The man fired two arrows into the bunny's chest, one after another. It screamed as it dropped to the ground. The oblong man pulled a mace and swung it at us.

The bowman grabbed my hand and pulled me. I didn't resist, though maybe I should have. I didn't know him any better than my pursuers, but at least he chose not to kill me, while the others were trying their best to do so.

"Where are we going?"

"Don't ask so many questions!" the man shouted as we broke through the brush. "Just run!"

The branches cut gashes in my arms and face. It seemed that the leaves were trying their best to hold us back, but we fought through them. The man was good at zigging and zagging through the canopy at full speed, preventing me from slamming into the verve by inches at every turn.

"In here," he said as we reached the sheer side of a cliff. I didn't see where he led us until the last moment, when the sides of a small cave made themselves known in the shadows.

He pulled me inside and clasped his hand over my mouth. There was silence so long that I nearly dropped my guard, but just as I thought about it, the oblong man stepped through the trees. It looked about for a long moment, then growled and turned away.

When the sounds stopped, the man let out a deep breath and dropped his hand. "You must be very valuable if a Seeker was sent for you. They do not sleep, or rest, until they find their target."

"Then why did it turn away?" I asked.

"It cannot be far from its totem, in this case, the rabbit."

"It was like no rabbit I have ever seen."

He nodded. "It is the kind of horror that this place breeds. If I had killed that rabbit, then the Seeker would have died with it, but since it still wanders the land, it means my shots were true enough to wound, but not kill."

"You saved me," I said, looking deep into his brown eyes. "You should be very proud of that."

"I still do not know if you are friend or foe, so I will save my pride until that becomes clear." He pushed himself up. "Come now. I have a place to rest and regain your strength."

CHAPTER 14
BETHEL

After meeting with the princesses, and Nimue, I took my leave, a thousand ideas rushing through my head.

I had survived so long without receiving Hastur's wrath because I knew how to play the game. I was more ruthless, loyal, and vicious than any of the other princesses, and that built up a small degree of leniency with the dark lord. He brutalized them, but he hadn't touched me in years, save for a tender moment on occasion.

Still, I knew what he was, a tyrant dictator who ruled by fear; one aroused by pain and suffering. Even though I never saw his wrath, my life was not a pleasant one, and I would not wish it on anyone. It meant walking a tightrope in a tornado, where not only any step you took could make you fall, but everything around you was conspiring to destroy you.

I found ways around being beaten and sodomized, but it meant making a thousand calculations every day. I provided Hastur with information to placate him and turn his attention away from me for a time, even if it meant affixing his gaze on the other wives and denizens of the castle.

Admittedly, I had betrayed those that never harmed me, and I even pointed the fingers to those Hastur favored best, hoping to gain his trust and transfer that love—no, it wasn't love so much as lack of hatred—to me. My lies were not even that convincing. I played each side against the other using all in my path, including my fellow princesses, as shields to protect me. Now I was being asked to work with those that I'd thrown to the wolves so many times.

As I walked through the palace, the thoughts of whether I could betray Hastur after all this time filled my mind. He must have known I was thinking about him because the demon statue next to me spoke, "Bethel, I would see you now."

My feet felt heavy on my way toward his quarters. I knew why he called me. The princesses meeting together for the first time in ages was curious at best and vexing at worst. He knew how powerful we were alone, and that together we might be the only force powerful enough to stop him in the whole of the Dark Planet. Together, we could guard him from even the likes of Baba and Rapunzel, but if we turned against him, we would be a problem.

The door to his quarters slammed shut when I entered. He stood before me with a glowing yellow robe and orange eyes that bore through my soul. "I heard you have agreed to be a bridesmaid for my beloved's wedding," he said, his voice a low growl.

I smirked. "Can we not lie to each other? I know you have no love for Nimue. This is but another game you play to amuse yourself."

He chuckled under his breath. I didn't often hear him laugh, and it was always cut off quickly. "You know me too well, better than any other in my orbit, which is why I need you to tell me the truth. Your meeting with Nimue, was there anything odd about it?"

"Nothing stranger than seeing my sisters in the same place together."

"I fear they will foment a plan against me," Hastur said. "Not all appreciate the power and safety I provide. Nimue is chief among them."

I stepped forward. "She is blind, but she will see the light, if you allow her to survive long enough to do so."

He grabbed a goblet, the same I had filled for him earlier, and took a drink. "My bride has made me a pact to keep her clean from wounds until our wedding night, but I do so much look forward to breaking her then."

"Will you kill her?"

"You know my proclivities, and how I get carried away, so I guarantee nothing, but I would much rather see this one broken than dead. She is so willful. To see her suffer under my boot, and then lick it, would be a glorious win for me. I have been so bored these years without a challenge."

"Is that why you agreed to her terms—boredom?"

He nodded. "She is full of fire and life. Just the thought of breaking her is a thrill."

"Of course, my lord." This was it. If I was going to turn on Nimue, it would be now or never. I would forever be cast into the fires with them, if somehow we succeeded. I bit my lip, feeling the heat of his gaze, and how violated it made me feel. It was horribly stupid, but I would do almost anything never to feel that again, even if it meant death, or worse. "I can tell you that they were quite catty, and we got nothing done. Aside from that, we only talked logistics. It was boring."

He nodded pensively, tapping his fingers against the

stem of the goblet. "If any other told me the same, I would not believe them, but since it is you—I will admit I am relieved."

"As you should be, my lord. If anything changes, I will let you know."

"Be sure that you do," he replied, finishing his wine. "And if I find out you are lying, then you will not like what I do to you, my favorite among princesses."

I bowed. "All I do is to make right by you."

"See that continues."

"Yes, my lord."

CHAPTER 15

ROSE

"Okay, I think I'm done," the healer Aziz said.

It had been the most excruciating thirty minutes of my life, but when I looked into the mirror my face was no longer bruised, and I was whole. I looked like I just went to the salon and got the works. "Did you get everything you need to tell Rama what happened to me?"

"Wh—I don—" He stopped, flustered.

"I know about healing, Aziz," I replied. "And it shouldn't hurt as much as you made it, unless you were searching for something. Is what I told you the truth? That I got into a fight with Kadlu and that's how I wound up with the brahmastra?"

"I don't know how you wound up with the weapon, but yes. You clearly got into a fight with Kadlu, and she gave you these bruises."

He wasn't lying, and neither was I, but it only told part of the story. "Then I think you should go. Tell Rama what you found out, and I never want to see you again."

"I don't work for you," he said in a snippy tone.

"No, you don't." I raised my hand and fire rose from it.

"But I have been blessed by two gods, and while I may not be as powerful as they are, I can fend for myself against the likes of you."

He jumped to his feet, bathed in fear, and scampered out the room. When the door opened, I noticed a tall, svelte Rama standing stoic on the other side of it. They spoke in hushed tones for a moment, then nodded to each other before going their separate ways; Aziz down the stairs, and Rama straight into my room.

"It's good to see you again." He looked over at the brahmastra. "I can't believe you found it. I have imagined this moment for a long time."

"Where is Chelle?"

"That is a delicate matter. You should recover your strength before—"

"I am perfectly fine," I replied, standing up to his level. "Where is Chelle? What have you done to her?"

He held up his hands. "She is fine. I talked to Odin this morning and he has agreed to release her soon. He just wants to run a couple of experiments on he—"

I stormed forward. "That's the love of my life! I don't care what you have to do. Get her back right now!"

"It doesn't work like that. These are the gods. They work on their own time horizon. If we poke Odin, he will retaliate, and it will not be pretty."

"Then I'll do it myself."

"You can't do that!"

I pushed past him, nudging his shoulder as I went. He stumbled slightly against my weight, like he had lost almost all his strength. Noting this, I stopped. "So, the bond worked. You really did lose your powers. I wasn't sure such magic would work on a god."

He nodded. "I was once a human, so that kind of magic is still pretty effective on me, and even more so now."

There was a sadness to his voice that I hadn't heard before. Even in his lowest moments, he still seemed in complete control, but now, he was very much afraid.

"I will not wait for long to rescue my love, and if he touches a hair on her head, I will slaughter him where he stands."

"He is coming for dinner. I think you will find him malleable to suggestion, especially from a beautiful woman."

"You want me to flirt with him?" My jaw dropped.

Rama stroked his chin, apparently considering this. "I want you to be polite. If all goes well tonight, not only will your beloved be returned, but we will also have the location of the key maker. You do remember that we were looking for him, too, in all this, so that we can save the universe."

"I don't care about any of that right now."

"Funny, because I thought that you turned your back on Chelle so you could help me save the universe."

"That was before I knew—" I was about to reveal what Kadlu had told me, but I held my tongue. If I hadn't given the powder to Red, I could have turned him right now. And if I hadn't promised Kadlu I would save him, I might have seriously considered snapping his neck where he stood.

"Make sure he brings Chelle to dinner."

"He'll never agree to that."

"Then make him!" I shouted. "I'm done playing with you. You are not the god you once were. Do not forget who holds the power here."

"I never will. It is neither you nor me. It is Odin. Don't you forget that. Now, I need to prepare. Will you excuse me, or would you continue to throw a pointless fit?"

As he spoke, I noticed something in his eyes. They dulled, only for a flash, and I swore that I saw something dart across them, from one to the other.

"Go," I replied with a growl.

He headed for the door. "Maricel made a delicious roast chicken. You should try it. Out of this world."

"I will consider it."

"See that you do," he replied. "Otherwise, it will all go to waste."

"Yes, we would hate for anything to go to waste, wouldn't we?" Like our entire plan. What a waste, if all we did was lose Chelle in the process and have to grovel to get her back. "That would be a shame."

CHAPTER 16

NIMUE

True to what I told Bethel, I was inundated with meetings all day. Florists, decorators, calligraphers, bakers, caterers, and about a hundred different people that flowed through the castle all needed to bend my ear about one thing or another. They scurried around like chickens with their heads cut off. I now knew the castle like the back of my hand, after weaving through it a dozen times while vendors followed, talking about their plans to transform the hall into a gothic masterpiece.

"Are you feeling okay?" a gnomish woman with a long, crooked nose asked. Her name was Flirget, and her boss ran events in the castle for seven years before his imprisonment after the unpleasantness of my attempted coup. Now, she held the mantle, and it didn't seem like she wanted it very much. I wouldn't either, of course. If things didn't go perfectly, she would be tortured—or worse.

"I am tired." I placed my fingers on my temples. "Can I have a break?"

She gave the wall a worried look. "We have a lot to get

through. I have our table vendor scheduled in five minutes."

Table vendor? "Why do we need a table vendor? Why is everything so complicated when it comes to weddings?" I fumed. "This insanity is why I never cared to marry. Many proposed, you know. I could have had my pick, but I told them no. I told them all no."

Flirget waited until I was calm again before she spoke. "Feel better?"

"No. That's why I need a break."

"We have a meeting in five minutes."

"You've said that," I spat. "Then, I will take four."

"We have much to do," she said. Her smile was tense. "But if you insist on being lazy and insulting our host, I can't stop you."

I had asked for a break several times since we began, but she clasped my arm each time, telling me that we had more important things to do than dilly dally. She was condescending every time she spoke to me, and I was sick of it.

"I do insist," I replied, leaning closer. "And please don't forget, if I survive my nuptials, and I certainly plan to, you will have more to worry about in Carcosa than a mad king. You will have a queen who knows very well how controlling you are, and how little respect you have for her."

Flirget sat up straight, pursing her lips. "You are not my client, despite the fact that you seem to have strong opinions on the proceedings. I work at the pleasure of the King in Yellow."

"Watch your tone," I replied. "I will be a full queen soon."

"If you live three days past the wedding, it will be a

miracle. I doubt you will last that long, given your constitution."

I stood from the hard chairs that made my legs go numb and headed to the gardens. "I will be in the garden. If I'm not back in four minutes, then wait longer. Do not disturb me."

"You had better hurry, because you only have three minutes now, and you had better believe I will come find you if you are a second late and report your insolence to Hastur myself."

She had no fear of saying the name. If anything, she hid behind it in case I had the insolence to take action against her.

"Try it, and he will kill you first, and I will laugh as you bleed to death at my feet."

It wasn't worth it to continue this contest with her. I would keep a list in my head of those who took the dark lord's side and be sure to take my vengeance against them if my plan happened to work, which seemed less likely by the second.

I thought that talking to the princesses would reveal a weakness in Hastur's defenses, but either they didn't know or wouldn't reveal a weakness beyond the one that laid behind a thick protection of thick armor he never removed.

At the moment, my best bet seemed to be a show of force, with the princesses bum-rushing him to the ground as I ripped the necklace holding Rapunzel's nose from his neck and stabbed him through the neck.

Outside, I walked to the grove of roses overlooking Carcosa. It was where we planned to hold the cocktail hour before the reception. The moment the florist showed me the view this morning, I fell in love with it. High trellises around the garden gave me some measure of privacy, and the long fall gave me a sense of relief, as if I could drop to my death at any time.

The wind whipped across my face as I looked out onto the land I would soon rule. Without Hastur's black ichor, I would not have been able to tolerate the movement of air across my body, but with the elixir I no longer felt like a raw nerve. Instead the wind felt like freedom, as though I could fly upon it and do anything.

"Hello, Nimue." It was the Faceless Woman, Rapunzel, made of the vines of the roses that surrounded the black trellises. "You are a hard woman to get a hold of."

CHAPTER 17

ROSE

As much as I wanted to spurn Rama's suggestion for food, I was deathly hungry. Culinary delights did not abound where I had been, living in the tunnels beneath Kadlu's world. I hadn't had a decent meal in days.

The kitchen was plastered with bright, brilliant white, from the wooden cabinets to the marble counters. The only bits of color were the stainless-steel appliances built into the walls.

"Good afternoon, Rose," Maricel said to me as I entered. Her red sari contrasted the rest of the kitchen and made her stand out against it like a vision. "How can I help you?"

Maricel had always been nice to me, and while her employer was a twat, I swallowed my anger at him so that I didn't transfer it to her. It wasn't her fault that her boss was a monster, was it?

"Rama said there was roast chicken. Is there any left?"

She nodded. "I'll make you a plate. You can go sit in the banquet room and I'll bring it to you."

I frowned. "Is there anywhere more...low key?" I

thought of the massive twenty-person oak table in the center of the room. "That place is way too fancy for me."

She pointed to a door on the other side of the kitchen. "There's a small eating area over there. It's meant for servants, but your friend Gabrielle likes it in there. She says it's quiet and peaceful, and I tend to agree. I am biased, of course."

I remembered that I had given Red my plastic bag. "Do you know where I might find her?"

"She was in the library the last I checked," Maricel said, arranging some potatoes on my plate.

I held up my finger. "Put a hold on that meal, Maricel. Something just came up."

"I'll keep it warm for you."

I thanked her and walked through the house until I found Gabrielle in the library, poring over a leather-bound book.

"What are you reading?" I asked, peeking over at the pages.

She looked up. "Fairy tales. Do you know the gods seeded them in every planet they created? The traditions changed in each star system, of course, as tales were told over and over again, and in different places of the universe, different stories took hold, but the bones of them all are the same."

"Is there a story about a little red hooded girl who goes to grandmother's house?" I asked, walking over to her.

"Blue hooded, actually, and it's her uncle's house in the original, but it's still recognizable."

"And the Emerald City?" I asked.

She shook her head. "That seems to come from the Dream Realm itself. That's probably where the blue hood became red, as I—well, as people slept and learned more about Urgu." She shrugged. "Or, at least that's my theory."

I sat down next to her. "It's as good a theory as any. At least it keeps your mind busy in this place."

"I try to." Red closed the book. "I get the feeling you aren't here to talk about fairy tales."

"Unfortunately not, but I like hearing about them all the same." I leaned closer. "Is there a place that's private we can talk safely, free of prying eyes and ears? I have something important to tell you."

"I know just the place."

Red grabbed my hand and stood, pulling me past the kitchen to a bare and confined hallway, at the end of which was a small room, dark and cramped. She closed the door and snapped the lock. The place barely fit the two of us.

"This is the furthest place in the mansion from Rama, and he never comes down here. The servant's quarters are no place for him."

"And what about Maricel?" I asked. "Will she pry?"

Red chuckled. "That's the best part. Maricel designed this room to scream in private. She doesn't like him any more than you do. If there is a safe place to speak in this place, then it is here." She reached into her pocket and produced the plastic bag filled with blue crystals. "Now, how about you tell me what this is, and what's going on."

I trusted Red completely, so there was no reason not to tell her everything, but something held me back. "Where did we first meet?"

Her eyes narrowed. "Are you really trying to test my loyalty to you?"

"After what I have learned, I need to know you are who you say you are."

"In the Dream Realm, outside of Critterton. You were kissing Chelle, if I remember. Good enough for you?"

I breathed a deep sigh of relief. "After what I have to tell you, you'll be thankful I was so careful."

"Then let's get on with it."

CHAPTER 18

BETHEL

What am I doing? I had just chosen to throw my lot in with usurpers instead of turning them in and saving my own skin. Just because Nimue spoke nice words and made me believe in her for a moment, because for that moment she made me believe that life could be different than a waking nightmare, I turned against everything I believed?

"Sister?" Elvira's red eyes looked through me, but she was surely talking to me. "May we speak in private?"

I hadn't spoken with her in years. We had been cordial enough during social occasions, but there was no love lost between us.

"Of course," I replied. "Lead the way."

There were places to speak in private if you knew the castle well enough, and we both knew it well. We walked outside to that thorny patch of briars that had once been a patch of roses before the blight caught it. No matter how many gardeners tried to revive the grounds, they never could find out what happened.

We knew, though. A graveyard of princesses and failed queens rested below our feet. The magic of the dead created a pocket where we could speak in private, away from the prying eyes of the staff. I had already been wary of conversing about our infidelity in the castle walls, and so I appreciated the extra layer of caution to protect us.

"What do you think of our queen?" Elvira asked. I appreciated that she did not beat around the bush about her motives. We were too powerful for such subversion, which made cavorting in secret all the more unsettling.

"I think she is well-intentioned," I replied. "And her words have a way of burrowing inside of you."

"Like maggots," Elvira said and shuddered. "We have never been in alignment in anything, and I fear that we welcome a bloodbath."

"I agree. The only thing that gives me solace is that all of us are on the same side for once. However, the balance is tenuous at best."

"That brings me to the heart of the matter," Elvira said. "We are the two most powerful of the king's princesses, and the idea of sharing power between the six of us, especially with a usurping queen, does not sit well with me. I look forward to the death of the dark lord as much as anyone, but—"

"But you want a bigger seat in the new world order," I said. She nodded. "I will be honest that I have thought the same. However, we must be careful how we proceed if we are to betray those we claim to work with."

I looked down at my arms. I was the only one who knew the spell Nimue cast was a farce. "Do you not fear reprisal should we betray our sisters?"

She shook her head. "We are still in concert against the dark lord. According to the pact we made, our vow is still valid."

It was a cunning deception. "I believe we should make an

accord. I fear others will be thinking the same, more than ready to take the crown from Nimue should she wield it. Better to have our own plan than to wait for others to carry theirs out."

"My thinking exactly."

"And what is your plan?"

"I have learned of a cursed object." She bit her lip. "I have actually known of it for a long time, but even with my great power, I cannot recover it alone. With it, we can kill the dark lord together, and take this world for our own."

Amazing. Nimue was right. One of us did have a secret way of killing Hastur. Perhaps there truly was more to her than meets the eye. Too bad she would not live to enjoy it should we defeat him.

"What is this object?"

Elvira paused, clearly wondering if this secret that she held was safe to share with me. Her lips pursed, and then opened several times, before she finally nodded.

"Long ago, when the king was young to this world, a powerful witch bound his heart inside of a golden locket. It rests at the bottom of a twisted prison at the heart of this world. He killed the witch once she performed the ritual, but I have communed with her in my dreams, and she has told me her sister can open the way forward to us."

"And who is her sister?" I asked.

"This is the part you will not like. She is the sister of Baba, the cursed witch."

I recovered quickly, but it had taken me aback. "She is our greatest enemy. Baba would never help us."

"The witch assured me that she will."

"And you trust her?"

"Yes, sister. I believe I do, but I know you are hesitant to do the same. It is why I brought you here." She knelt and drew a summoning circle under her. "We are about to meet her, if I have done the spell correctly."

She placed her hands on either side of the circle and muttered a curse under her breath. The circle glowed and from its center, a blue spirit rose into the air. The woman's image whose light flickered on to us was the spitting image of Baba, except younger, with kinder eyes.

"It is about time," the ghost growled. "I thought you would never come for me."

"I'm sorry, Issha. It took me longer than I thought to choose a partner for the journey."

Issha looked me over and sneered. "And you chose this waif of a thing. We are truly doomed."

I stepped forward. "Do not speak to me, specter, as if I am a brittle thing. I will destroy you where you stand."

She sighed. "If only that were possible, but I can only rest once my shame is destroyed."

Elvira knit her eyebrows. "Then that is why you are helping us?"

"It is," she replied. "Once the king is dead, I can finally find peace."

"Then tell us how to convince your sister to help us," I said. "We are her sworn enemies."

"There is a tree in the forest where I used to live. Inside of it is a letter I wrote many centuries ago. Find it and bring it to my sister. If that doesn't convince her, then nothing will."

"And if nothing will..." I said.

"Then we are all doomed," Issha replied. "Especially the two of you, because if the King in Yellow does not die, he will discover your plot, and I fear you will suffer more greatly than any other."

"Brilliant." I rolled my eyes. "Sounds like it will be no trouble whatsoever."

"It is worth the risk," Issha said. "For once the heart is returned to the king's body, he will be vulnerable, and you can slaughter him. It is the only thing that can."

"Why would you do such a thing?"

"We did not know he would be so vicious when we made him, and I had a bigger heart than my sister. I believed that the King in Yellow could save the world instead of condemning it. I was a naïve fool, as the young often are."

I stared at the ghost while I mulled all of it over. "Are you sure this will work?"

"I created him myself, so I know his weakness better than anyone."

"Then I suppose we will trust you, as we have no other choice," I growled. "So help me if you are lying to us, I will find a way to capture you and torture you the rest of my days."

CHAPTER 19

RED

After Rose finished her story, I stared at her in silence for a long moment. "So, Rama has been infected by an alien parasite, and you are taking all of this from a woman who is his known enemy?"

"She's not an enemy of Rama. She loves him."

"Right, and she told you this before she beat you senseless...because you asked her to?"

Rose nodded. "That's right."

I pressed my fingers to the bridge of my nose. "Do you understand how insane that sounds?"

Rose pulled my hand down so she could look me in the eyes. "Everything that has happened to me in the past couple of years has been insane. I fell into the Dream Realm. I became a queen. I saved the Underworld. I pulled my girlfriend back from the dead. We are standing in the frigging Celestial Realm, in the house of a god. You're telling me this is any crazier than that?"

"Yes, I am, which should tell you exactly how off the wall your story is."

Rose held out her hand. "If you don't believe me, then give me back the bag and I'll do it myself."

"Are you crazy?" I asked, squeezing the blue bag tighter. "This could be poison. It could be anything. I'm not just going to let you blow it in Rama's face. What if it hurts him?"

"What if it saves him?" Rose folded her arms across her chest. "What then?"

I put my hand on her shoulder. "All right, look. I'm not saying you're completely off the rails, but I have to think about this for a moment. Maybe there's a way to prove that Rama is what you say that he is."

"And if I can prove it, then will you give me back the cure?"

"Yes. If you can prove that Rama is infected with some evil spore and that this stuff isn't going to kill him, then I'll give it back to you. Meanwhile, I have to see a man about a key."

Rose's hand dug into my arm. "If he's evil, which he is, then whatever he's planning to do with the Dark Planet can't be trusted."

"That's where Nimue is, Rose. The woman who took everything from me, and who's tried to kill you more times than I can count." My breath came out in a huff. "I'm going there, and I'm going to kill her."

"And what if you loose something horrible on the universe by opening that door?"

I leaned in until my face was nearly touching hers. "Let me go, or I will make you."

She dropped her hand. "I am a queen, Red, blessed by two gods. Not some fragile thing. If I wanted that bag, I would take it, but I need you to trust me."

"Then come up with something less crazy. I don't trust Rama either, but he's proven himself a good friend."

Rose looked exasperated, maybe hurt. "And what type of friend am I?"

"The best kind," I replied. "Which is why I have to make sure you're not going to ruin everything by following some hairbrained idea told to you by somebody you shouldn't trust."

Her eyes narrowed. "I thought you knew me better than that."

"I do, and I know when you are acting irrational."

I left her before she could answer. I had read about something called Stockholm Syndrome, where you begin to trust and identify with your captors. Rose was certainly suffering from something similar, but she was right. She wasn't some fragile thing. I had followed her into battle, and across the universe. If she believed that Rama was evil, then I owed it to her to investigate.

By the time I got back upstairs to the kitchen, Rama was sitting at the island eating a plate of roasted chicken. "Didn't you just eat?" I asked.

He shoveled another pile of food into his mouth. "You humans have to eat all the time."

"Tell your friend," Maricel said from the far end of the room. "I gave her plate to Master Rama, but I will fix her another when she comes back."

I turned back to the door. "She'll be along soon, but I'm not sure if she'll be in the mood to eat anymore."

"Did you get into a fight?" Rama asked, not bothering to swallow his food before he spoke.

"Something like that."

"A lover's quarrel?"

I chuckled. "If you knew how much she loved Chelle, you wouldn't say that."

"I've loved many women, and that never stopped me from taking a lover. Kadlu thought it was one of my best qualities, to be so full of love for everyone I met."

"Chelle would not be so understanding." I slid in next to him. "Why does Kadlu hate you now, if she once loved you?"

Rama shrugged. "I don't know. One day she just got very violent, said I wasn't myself, and had it out for me. I swear she tried to kill me a half dozen times before I finally ran off. That's when I left my weapon behind." He leaned into me after swallowing a mountain of food. "Food was never this good as a god. It's the one thing I enjoy about being a human."

I leaned back in my chair, trying to size him up. "Rose thinks you tried to kill her in order to get to Kadlu. Is that true?"

"Of course not." He placed his hand on my knee. "Your friendship is everything to me, and I know how much you care about her."

I watched his eyes for a long moment and swore I saw something dash from one side of them to the other, darting between them like a tadpole. It was exactly as Rose said. It didn't mean she was right, but there was something odd there.

"I hope you believe me," Rama said, "because you mean a great deal to me."

I don't know what to believe. "I do. Of course I do."

CHAPTER 20

ARIEL

I never needed sleep like I did in the Nightmare Realm. Nevertheless, I followed the hunter back through the cave until our path rose up a steep incline. He made it up the sheer cliff, but I slid and would have tumbled all the way back to the bottom if he hadn't reached down and latched on to my hand.

"I got you," he replied, and pulled me up to the landing.

I was surprised to find a sleeping bag there, plus a small fire pit with a kettle on it and several pairs of clothes. I was less surprised to find a cache of weapons.

"It's not much," he said. "But it's home. Back on Earth I had a nice flat and all the amenities, but I'm not on Earth anymore, am I?"

I sat in the cramped space. "How long have you been here, er—what's your name?"

"Corben," he replied. "What's yours?"

"Ariel," I said. "Funny, you saved me and didn't know my name, and I followed without knowing yours."

"You're lucky I ran into you," he said. "There are plenty

of monsters worse than that Seeker and its rabbit companion."

"How long have you survived here?"

He shrugged. "I don't know. When I left Earth, it was 1995."

"That is a far cry less time than I have been stuck in the Dream Realm."

"When did you come to Urgu, then?"

"It's hard to remember the exact date, but I believe it was 1783, or thereabouts. The trouble in the colonies had just ended, that I remember vividly."

He chuckled. "So, my country barely existed when you came here. I have to say, you look good for a two-hundred-year-old."

I smiled at him. "Thank you. It's all in the genes, you see."

I chuckled at the ridiculousness of my words after I said them, and he did, too. It was nice to laugh with somebody again. I hadn't done it much in the last several hundred years. Everything had been terrible for so long that I wasn't even sure I could laugh anymore, and here it burst forth from me.

Corben let out a sigh. "We should not be so loud, or they will hear us. The caves have ears, and mouths that echo."

"I'm sorry," I replied. "I don't have much occasion for levity these days."

"I understand that."

I looked over against the wall and saw a second sleeping bag, wrapped up tightly and leaning against the rock. "Is there somebody else that lives here with you?"

He shook his head. "Not anymore. She was taken...like so many of my friends have been."

"By the Shadow King?"

He studied his hands. "Things were not well before he came to power, but now, it is so much worse. We used to have a place in the mountains where we were safe. It was a beacon of hope for us, but then, it was raided, and we all dispersed to the winds. Many of us were caught. The lucky among us fled and found solace elsewhere. Since then, the Seekers have tried to track us all down. I don't know what the Shadow King has planned for us, but I have no intention of finding out. Of all the places in Sprig, you must stay away from his palace most of all."

"That's funny," I replied. "Not laughing funny, but ironic funny."

"What is?"

"Hypnos, the god of my planet, told me to follow the strongest beings in Sprig to find the eye, and if he is to be believed, then it would seem I need to travel to the Shadow King's castle and seek out my fortunes from him."

A shadow passed over Corben's face. "You should never go there, ever."

"I cannot get back to my home without the eye, and my patron's words lead me there," I said. An idea came to me then. "Hey, why don't you help me?"

"Now that is laughable," he replied with a chuckle.

"No, it's not. Come with me. We can save your friends, and I can bring you all back to Urgu, where you'll be safe."

He bit his lip. "Don't promise things you can't deliver."

"I can deliver it." I placed my hand on his. He jerked back, then relaxed slightly. "I promise. If you help me recover the object I need, then I will bring your friends home."

Corben's eyes looked glassy. He smiled. "It has been so

long since I've had hope, I'm not sure what to do with it now."

"Hold it close," I replied. "It is everything."

He hesitated before speaking again. "Very well, if you can do what you say, then I will help you, but do not deceive me."

"Never."

Still watching me intently, he said, "I will take first watch. You can sleep as long as you like. I don't need much of it these days."

I curled up in his sleeping bag without question, and drifted off to sleep without a second thought, or a fear in my head. With Corben taking care of me, I truly believed that I was safe.

CHAPTER 21
NIMUE

"What do you want, Rapunzel?" I growled as I spurned her visage in the rose vines outside of Hastur's castle. In reality, she had no facial features, but the red blooms she inhabited formed her eyes and lips. The small and dainty nose looked just like the one Hastur wore around his neck.

"Is that any way to treat an old friend?" she said.

"Friends don't send friends to their deaths."

The rose petals turned downward into a frown. "That wasn't my fault. Cassandra deceived me the same she did you, and now, my little birdies tell me you have learned to trust her again." Her red eyes looked me up and down. "Even after what she has done to you."

"I worry constantly about her stabbing me in the back before my plans come to fruition, but I don't have many other options for confidants around here. In fact, she has been an invaluable asset."

She studied the horizon. "Yes, I have learned you still plan to kill the yellow king. This pleases me."

"How do I know it is truly you, and not an illusion conjured by my betrothed?" The last time the Faceless

Woman appeared to me, it turned out to be a trick of Hastur's, born from his deceit and malice.

"Ask me something only I would know."

I searched my memory. "What were the first words you spoke to me?"

Without a moment's hesitation, her lips parted. "I asked 'Do you submit?' to which you responded 'I do. I do,' like a pathetic child. Look at what you have become since then."

"No thanks to you," I said. "After torturing me those first days after I arrived on this planet, you stayed silent for a month, saying nothing, doing nothing to help me, until the day I could be of use to you."

"I'm sorry you feel that way," Rapunzel said. "I was trying to teach you patience, and you were a very bad student. You seem to prefer going out on your own and improvising, even if it ends with the skin ripped from your body."

"I never did well in school or as a servant. I prefer to blaze my own path, burning down those that stand against me."

"Yes, that does sound like you." She turned to face me again. "Do you believe that I am who I say I am?"

"I do, and yet, it brings me no comfort."

"Why is that?" Rapunzel asked. "Do you not think me an ally to you?"

"I don't know what you are to me," I replied. "But when I look at you, my stomach ties itself into knots."

The petals around her eyes narrowed. "That is because you still owe me the gift of my nose, and the guilt eats at you."

I nodded. "Perhaps that is it."

"You should not fear my wrath or keep guilt buried

deep in your soul. All will be forgiven with the death of the yellow king, when you pull my nose from his dead carcass." She smiled. "The thought of it pleases me greatly."

"I'm not doing any of this for you," I growled.

"As long as he is out of my way, and I recover the piece of my face he stole"—a hand of flowers appeared and touched the button nose—"I don't really care why you are doing it."

"You will have your nose, woman, though if you can simply grow one out of flowers, I don't know why you don't." I huffed. "The rest of your face won't be found so easily."

She waved me off with her flowery hand. "Don't worry yourself about those trivialities. I have others working on that around the cosmos. You simply need to give me the piece of my face we agreed on, and I will honor my promise to make you more powerful than you could ever imagine."

I leaned closer to her. "If I kill the dark lord, I will accomplish that without your help. I will still honor our deal because I want peace in the new world order that I create."

"Then you aim to be queen?"

"I aim to share power with those that have been wronged by the King in Yellow, yes, and create a better world from the ashes of the old one."

"Baba won't like that," Rapunzel replied. "You made a deal with her."

"A deal born of manipulation." I shook my head. "I have no remorse bowing out of her ill-obtained deal that should never have been made in the first place."

"Baba will not see it that way."

"Then I will count on my new ally to keep her in line, won't I?"

"You expect me to keep Baba in line?" She chuckled. "You were my student not long ago, and now you speak to me as an equal."

"I am every bit your equal," I spat back. "If not in raw power, then in stature. Look at what I have done with nothing. If you gave me all you know, this whole world would submit to me."

"They might yet," she replied with a slight tip of her floral head. "Which is why I suppose there is every reason to help you."

Footsteps clomped through the garden, and I peered through the trellis to see Flirget headed over. I had used more than my allotted three minutes, and she was coming to exert what little power she had over me.

"Our next meeting has arrived. You are needed inside."

"Coming," I said, and headed back towards the castle. I looked back over my shoulder, but Rapunzel's face had vanished, and the roses were twisted back to their original form.

CHAPTER 22
ARIEL

I woke with a start when Corben slammed his hand down on my mouth and pressed his finger to his lips. He pointed over to the edge of the cave, where the Seeker and its disgusting rabbit familiar inched forward.

"We have to go," Corben whispered.

I slid carefully out of the sleeping bag, my breath shaky. He grabbed his bow and quiver and handed me a small dagger that felt awkward in my hand. I had rarely wielded a weapon before, aside from my magic.

Corben slid a longsword into his belt and then drew another one. With a deep breath, he heaved it over the edge. It clattered in the distance, and the Seeker perked up and rushed toward the sound.

"Come on." Corben grabbed my hand and helped me down the cliff face.

"Why can't we stay here where it is safe? That beast is too big to reach us here."

"Have you ever been treed before?" he asked. I shook my head. "It's when a predator gets you alone in a tree, and then just has to wait until you fall from exhaustion or starve. If we stay here, we'll be safe enough for a time, but we'll be sitting ducks. Better to move into the open where we stand a chance of escaping."

I didn't ask more questions, though I had many. I was too afraid our whispers would bounce off the caves into our enemy's ears.

Corben made it down to the flat ground first and held out his hands to help me. However, when I reached for him, I tumbled. Rocks slid down and erupted with the noise. For a moment there was no noise, but then a loud shriek went out across the air, filling my ears and causing my body to bristle.

"The rabbit is alerting the Seeker of prey."

Sure enough, I caught a glimpse of the rabbit pointing at us and screeching. The Seeker turned in our direction. Corben pulled out a pair of arrows and fired them at the lumbering oaf. One of the arrows missed completely, but the other lodged in its shoulder. The Seeker ambled forward as if it hadn't been hit at all.

"Get behind me."

I leapt to the other side of Corben as he pulled out the longsword and hacked at a netting I hadn't noticed before. With the third swing, the rope dislodged, releasing a cavalcade of rocks that crashed into the Seeker. The bunny hopped onto a craggily ledge to avoid being trampled.

Corben grabbed my arm and pulled me away. My feet turned faster than I knew how to move, stumbling on the uneven ground.

"It's too quick!" I shouted, tripping again.

He pulled me to my feet as the Seeker stomped toward us again. Corben fired two more arrows into its knees, but the monster took no notice.

"You have to move faster, Ariel. These monsters will not

let up until they have you in their paws, and you are the property of the Shadow King."

I nodded, gasping to catch my breath. "I will, I promise."

I wasn't sure I could fulfill my oath to Corben, but he could have left me to face my fate in the woods and didn't. Instead, he brought me to his home, and now it would never be safe again. The least I could do was move faster to avoid being captured. Still, my feet did not want to cooperate. As we moved, they twisted and slid until, as Corben leapt across a ditch between two outcroppings of rock, they gave out completely. I fell into the ravine with a shriek.

"Ariel!" he shouted and held out his hand.

I tried to reach him, but it was no use. He was too high up, even after he held down his bow for me to grab hold of.

The cries of the rabbit closed in, and I could tell by Corben's face that the Seeker wasn't far. "I'll find some rope to get you out."

I shook my head. "No, you have to keep going. Leave me here."

"I'm not leaving you!"

"We barely know each other. Don't be a hero. Save yourself. I'll be fine."

His jaw muscles clenched, and he spoke through gritted teeth. "You absolutely won't be fine, Ariel. That's the whole damned point. These beings are—"

"I know what they are!" I screamed. "Live to fight another day. I'm going to get captured. I've made my peace with that, but I won't take you down with me. Now go!"

He looked up and his eyes went wide, and then down at me. "I'll find you again. I'm sorry."

"Just run!"

Corben took one last look at me, and then he was gone.

The Seeker came into view, took one step toward him, and then the rabbit shrieked again.

"He's nothing! The girl is what matters." The rabbit hopped across the chasm and stared at me. "That is a mighty tough predicament you've gotten yourself into, isn't it?"

"Don't gloat," I replied with a snarl. "It's unbecoming."

"Oh, I don't care about such things. That's the advantage of being in the Nightmare Realm. No rules. You would like it, maybe, if you got to know it. Unfortunately, I don't think there's much chance you'll enjoy the Shadow King, especially given where you're from."

The Seeker's arms extended down and wrapped around me. I hacked away at them with my dagger, but no matter how many times I cut them, they grew again, until, eventually, the Seeker smacked away the blade and held my arms against my body. I struggled, but I was nothing compared to the strength of the demonic monster.

The Seeker raised me into the air until I was face to face with the rabbit, who stunk of rubbing alcohol. Two murky eyes poked out of its head and its teeth were yellowed and pointy. The rest of him was patchy, gnarled fur.

"The more you struggle, the more fun we get to have," it said with a sick smile. "So please, wriggle away."

The rabbit nodded at the Seeker, who squeezed me until I could barely breathe, and the fight left me. I was their prisoner now, but the joke was on them. The place they planned to take me was exactly where I wanted to go.

CHAPTER 23

ROSE

Red denied me. She was my only friend in all of this, the only person I could trust, and she didn't believe I aimed to save Rama, not destroy him. She thought I had been tricked by Kadlu's words. It gave me pause to wonder if she even knew me at all. I had sparred with gods before, some many times more cunning and powerful than Kadlu, and they hadn't duped me. Why didn't she have faith in me?

I could have taken the crystals by force, but I didn't want it to come to that. Even if saving Chelle was my first priority, I hated the idea of injuring Gabrielle to do it. Chelle would, too. I was pacing back and forth across the study when Maricel came to find me. She waited until I noticed her.

"Yes, Maricel?" I asked once I finally did. "How can I help you?"

She had a sweet smile. "I need to go to the store to pick up some ingredients for tonight. Would you like to come with me?"

"Can't you just magic up everything you need?"

She held out her hands. "I could, but the taste is not the

same as fresh ingredients, and Lord Odin will know the difference. Rama does not like to accompany me on such errands, but I could use another set of hands to help carry the bags."

The hopefulness in her voice was what threw me. Maricel never asked for anything from me and from her tone it seemed that there was something more to her ask than wanting the poor company I could provide.

"I am happy to help, but I am a wanted woman out in the world."

She held up a necklace that I recognized. It was the one that Rama used to conceal himself from all he didn't want to know his dealings. "I think I can help with that," she said.

"How did you get this?"

"I have access to all of Rama's things, and he hasn't needed this much since he became an acting member of the Board. I thought perhaps you could use it." She placed the necklace in my outstretched palm.

I finished with the clasp and traced the necklace on my skin. "Thank you. It simplifies things if I can't be seen."

"We can't have you getting arrested for helping me, can we? Rama would never let me hear the end of it."

I had never gotten a good look at the exterior of Rama's house. The last time I entered, I was unconscious, and the time before we had entered through a magical portal. His home sat high atop a hill that looked down over the whole of the Celestial Realm. It was a nice mansion, but far from the only of its kind. Several others lined the horizon, each with its own spectacular view.

I stared at them a long moment, ruminating. "What kind of god do you have to be to construct a house like Rama's?"

Maricel waited until we were through the gate to answer. "A vain one."

My eyebrows shot up. I had never heard the woman utter a bad word about her boss in all my time knowing her. "I'm frankly a little surprised you said that."

"It's no surprise that I think him vain. He would admit it himself. The most powerful gods in the universe can manipulate anything, and their homes in the Celestial Realm are an embodiment of their ego."

I looked out over the homes and apartments in the valleys below. "I'm surprised every god does not have a similar mansion, then."

Her smile was cracked with pain. "You don't know much about us, Rose, so I won't hold it against you that you insult my people like that."

"You?" I asked. "You're a god?"

"A minor one, and there are exponentially more like me than like Rama. Ones that don't have infinite power and are humble in our aims. You happen to have met some of my strongest kin in your travels, but most of us desire to have a simple life."

"But not Rama."

She began walking and jerked her head, indicating that I should come along. "He desires power above all else. Even at his best, he seeks it always."

"He is not so powerful now, is he?" I asked. "Now that he is a mortal."

Maricel turned to me. "Please, I beg you. Do not say such things. If it got out that he was— well, he would be in great danger."

"That is not my goal." I slowed my pace. "I want to help him."

"I know you do." She took a deep breath. "Did you know that Kadlu was my sister?"

I came to a stop. "I had no idea."

"Once she betrayed Rama, the whole realm turned on us. Our planets were stripped away, and the Board took our land."

"Can't you just make new land? You are gods, after all."

Maricel resumed walking. "It is not so easy for all of us. We do not have the power of creation. We relied on the kindness of the Board to increase our holdings, and when they turned against us—it was not good. The rest of my family was confined to the Crystal Keep, but I—Rama made a special dispensation to keep me free, as his servant." She cleared her throat. "I thought it was a kindness, but he is cruel and distant, and now I know that he wanted me to watch him drag my sister's name through the mud, powerless to do anything about it."

I wanted so badly to tell Maricel what I knew, but she had served Rama for too long for me to loosen my lips. "I'm sorry that happened to you, that it keeps happening to you."

"You have met her. Please, tell me about my sister. I know she held you captive, but you must have learned something about her before you escaped."

"I—she didn't—she would—" I caught myself. Maricel was kind, but I could not risk my secret. "I don't think I can say any more about her than what I have already told, so if you brought me out here to learn more, then I'm afraid you are going to be sorely disappointed."

She sniffled and wiped her eyes. "Please, if there is anything. You have no idea what it would mean."

"No." I looked away. "I do not trust you, Maricel. I am sorry for it, but that is the truth."

"I understand." Now it was her turn to stop. She licked her lips. "The room you spoke to Gabrielle in was not as soundproof as I led her to believe. I heard everything you said, and if I wanted to betray you, then I would have done so to Rama already."

"I...don't believe you."

"Why do you think that I brought you here? I wanted you to trust me and tell me what you knew freely, but now I know how you feel about me, and that is good to know." She reached into her pocket and pulled out the blue crystals. "Will this really save Rama from the horrors that have eaten at him for so long?"

My jaw dropped. "How did you get that?"

"I can go unnoticed when I choose. Gabrielle is not the only one with that skill. I heard you talking, and I took it for myself. I can give it back to you, if I like the answer to my question. Now, please let me know what my sister told you about these crystals."

"Of course." I nodded, still dumbfounded. "According to Kadlu, one crystal will be enough to turn Rama back into the god you once knew."

She squeezed the crystals. "Then I have the perfect meal. We will mix it in his food and save him."

"You don't have to do this. Red wasn't wrong. It might kill him. I am only going on what Kadlu said. She might have been lying."

"She wasn't." Maricel set her jaw. "I trust my sister with my life, and I will trust her with Rama's, too."

CHAPTER 24

BETHEL

The door to the castle swung open and the new event coordinator stomped into the small cliffside garden. Elvira quickly dispelled the summoning circle and Issha vanished. Moments later, Nimue appeared on the path, following Flirget back to the castle.

"Flirget looks mad," I muttered to Elvira.

"Like her predecessor. Though I suppose I would be mad too if I had to plan a wedding in two days."

I chuckled. "Do you remember how mad she would get if we were seconds late to our cue?"

"In fairness, she was imprisoned after the last fiasco so maybe her fear was founded."

"I have had occasion to torture her. She is not so tough."

"Tell me about it." A smile crept onto Elvira's face. "I do get pleasure out of listening to her beg, though, after all she said to us over the years."

"There are many things I dislike about the dark king's reign, but torturing infidels is not one of them."

"I agree." Elvira gave me a conspiratorial smile.

Flirget stalked back to the castle after exchanging some

words with Nimue near the trellis. The future queen slid out from behind the verve and followed the wedding planner. I had need of Nimue if we were going to be able to leave the castle long enough to track down the golden locket Issha talked about. The other princesses would have to cover for us, and Nimue would have to lie.

I caught up with her quickly. "May I speak with you?"

She turned to me. "Ah, Bethel. Of course."

"No!" Flirget shouted, wheeling around. "We have appointm—"

Elvira held up a finger. "Do not ever raise your voice to us, lest you want to feel the same wrath as your predecessor."

Flirget swallowed hard. "I suppose I can get started without you, Nimue. Come presently when you are able."

"Absolutely," Nimue grumbled, watching Flirget stomp back into the castle. "I hate her so much. It takes all my power not to ring her neck."

"That might endear you to the yellow king," I said.

"It would certainly endear you to me," Elvira added.

"That almost makes it worth it on its own." A sneaky smile rose on Nimue's face. "How can I help you?"

Elvira looked at me, and then back at Nimue. "We have need to leave the castle on a special mission, and the dark lord must not know of our plans."

"If I am to lie for you, I will need more details."

I craned my neck around, checking for spies, before I continued to talk. "It is not safe to discuss openly, as you can imagine, but it is of utmost need to succeed in our aims. I dare say it would be impossible to achieve what we seek without it. Wouldn't you agree, dear sister?"

Elvira nodded. "I would say it's critical, but we cannot say more, for creeping eyes are everywhere." Nimue and I followed her gaze to see Flirget staring out the window at us. "See what I mean?"

"I have no choice but to trust you." Nimue stroked her chin. "I can say you went to acquire a wedding present for us, or for me, as my bridesmaids."

An idea came to me. "There is a tradition in the Northern Isles of carrying carrion flowers down the aisle. They only grow in one grove in the north country, where I am from. I can bring some back for you to cover your story."

Nimue nodded. "That would be lovely. How could I get married without carrion flowers? I am shocked I have not been privy to such a thing in all my meetings."

"The florists in this castle could not hold a candle to those of my hometown," I said. "We had a tradition of supplying royal weddings back to the beginning, until the dark lord did away with all royalty save for himself."

"I will cover for you," Nimue stepped forward, waving a finger at me. "I do not know what you are planning, but I am already wary. I am hanging this alliance together with blood and bone, and I fear you work to fracture it."

Elvira placed her hands on Nimue's shoulder. "If we wanted to betray you, we would have already done so. If we wanted to kill you, we would have had ample opportunity. We do not need circuitous methods or lies to make that happen, and our gracious king would commend us for doing it, especially after he learned of your treachery."

Nimue pulled Elvira's hands off her shoulder. "You think me weak because I have been laid low, but that I still draw breath proves my strength. You hide behind your power, while I stand proudly behind my weakness." She began to walk away. "I will cover for you, but you must be back by the time of the wedding, or my betrothed's ire will never be satiated."

Nimue turned to walk away, finally disappearing through the door and pulling Flirget from her post.

"I can't believe I'm saying this," Elvira said, staring after the future queen. "But I think I like her."

I smirked. "It's okay, sister. I like her, too. That might be the only reason she's still walking. Now, let us go do what must be done and take our rightful place on the throne."

"Yes, sister. That sounds like a capital idea."

CHAPTER 25

RED

I searched through the whole house, including the servant quarters, searching for Rose. The way I ended it with her didn't sit right with me.

"What are you looking for?" Rama finally asked me as I passed him for the tenth time. He was in the game room, content to play pool with himself as he waited to change for dinner.

"Rose," I replied, walking into the room.

"She left with Maricel." Rama knocked the cue ball into the 9 and watched it roll perfectly into the pocket.

"What?" I replied, spinning toward the exit. "She can't go out there. She's a wanted woman."

"Relax," Rama said, taking another shot and sinking the 10 and 3 balls. It didn't seem to matter to him that one was stripes and the other solids. "Maricel gave her my amulet, so nobody will be able to recognize her except for people who I've allowed to see me, which isn't many people. Certainly none who wish her harm."

My brows furrowed. "I don't understand. Why would they both leave? Rose barely knows Maricel."

Rama shrugged. "She said she needed help with groceries for tonight. I don't ask questions."

There was something strange going on, but I couldn't put my finger on it. Now that I suspected Rama, I couldn't confide my fears in him, which meant I had to push my suspicions down into my gut.

"I'm glad you're here," Rama said, walking his cue to a rack that housed many others. "Odin called and told me that he had tracked down the key maker and didn't want to make me wait until dinner to fetch it. Can you be a dear and go get it for me?"

"Don't you want me here for protection?"

He laughed. "Rose is much better protection that you, my dear. She's been blessed by two gods, and you have been blessed by none. Being good with weapons isn't helpful around one of the most powerful gods in the universe."

I pulled the golden dagger from its hilt. "I still have this that can kill a god. Can Rose do that?"

"Yes, you are very scary, but I have use of you elsewhere," Rama said. "You'll go right from Odin's to find the key maker, so bring the brahmastra and the dagger. I don't know how much of the material he'll need to make a duplicate."

"And what if he doesn't want to make a new key?" I asked. "What if he went into hiding for a reason?"

"Then I believe you have a golden dagger that can kill a god." His voice was cold and distant. "Impress on him what will happen to him if he doesn't comply."

"I'm not a bully."

Rama gave me a disgusted look. "Of course you are. A glorified one, sure, which allows you to sleep at night. Don't get it twisted, though. You impose your will on others to get what you want. We just don't call it being a bully in polite society."

"And what do you call it, then?"

"Guard? Spy? Hero? Oh mercy, there are just so many ways to call a bully a bully while making it more palatable."

I stepped forward. "You're not making me want to help you very much, right now."

He shrugged. "It doesn't matter, because you will anyway."

"Why do you say that?"

"Because getting that key is the only way you get to kill Nimue, and isn't that what all this is for?"

He was right, but still I sneered. "You are on thin ice."

He leaned back against the pool table. "I'm sorry I'm telling you things you don't like to hear. The truth is never easy when you've shrouded yourself in pleasant lies."

I squeezed the hilt of the golden dagger. "You know I can slit your throat, right?"

"I am a mortal. Killing me isn't very hard. A well-trained gerbil, or a poorly eaten piece of candy can do that, too." He shooed me out. "Now, go. We don't have a moment to spare if we hope to save the universe."

"You're a dick."

"Yes, yes. Sticks and stones and the like. Now, have a good trip, and don't return without that key."

As I moved out of the room, I wondered if he was really trying to save the world or damn it to destruction. Either way, he was right. I would help him, because more than anything I wanted to put Nimue in her place, consequences be damned. I had worked too hard for too long to bring my vengeance down upon her, and nothing was going to stop me.

"I hate you."

"You love me." He smiled. "That's the hardest pill for you to swallow."

CHAPTER 26

ARIEL

The rope the Seeker bound me with was coarse on my neck and arms. With every step we took through the woods, I half-expected Corben to leap out and save me, but it was a fool's hope. I wished him far away from danger. I had told him to leave me and meant it; the last thing I wanted was for him to perform a daring escape and risk himself. Besides, I would soon be in front of the exact person I needed to see in order to save Urgu, or at least that was my hope.

"Drop her here," the rabbit said. The Seeker threw me against a rock in a clearing.

A huge castle loomed on top of a gnarled hill. "Is that where we're going?"

"Shut up," the rabbit growled as he gathered kindling for a fire. "Don't make me gag you."

"I'm sorry," I replied. "I'm not trying to cause trouble. I'm new here, which is why I'm asking for your help in understanding this place."

The rabbit's whiskers twitched. "Yeah, that's where we're going; the Shadow King's castle. I've already sent word to expect us, so don't get any bright ideas. If you disappear, he'll send a thousand like me to find you."

"Why am I so special?"

He arranged the sticks in a pile and used two rocks to create a spark. "Most of us remember the Dream Realm from Epiales's war with his brother, and how beautiful it was. When the Shadow King came to power, he promised us to open the portal again, but it's been years now and he hasn't delivered. You're the first bit of hope he's had in a long time."

"Urgu will not fall again. We are better prepared than last time."

The rabbit laughed. "That's a good one. If there's one thing I know for sure, it's that people that live in places like Urgu are fat and lazy. They have no interest in doing the hard work of preparing for a war, while we are hardened like stone."

I raised my eyebrows. "You might be right. Honestly, I have not been on the surface long enough to confidently back up my claims. Still, if you believe I can help you open a portal to the Dream Realm, you will find my value lacking. Hypnos opened the portal for me, and there's nothing that I can do to open it again."

"The Shadow King will find a way. I can smell the god's power on you from here, and if you have his power flowing through your veins, then my boss will find a way to extract it."

We stayed silent for a long time after that, as I watched the rabbit cook a twisted version of pheasant over the fire. When it was done, the rabbit leaned back against a smooth rock.

"Do you have to eat?" I asked. "We don't have to eat in Urgu."

"You ask a lot of questions." He looked back at the Seeker. "I guess it's not so bad, though, given as my partner doesn't speak much."

"Must be lonely."

"It's okay," he replied. "Better than when I was powerless, I guess. At least people don't mess with me. Now, I get to be the one doing the chasing."

"It must be hard, being in Sprig. It seems like everything wants to kill you every minute of every day."

"That's why it's better to be the hunter than the hunted." He looked down at the remains of the desecrated pheasant. "No, I don't have to eat. I do it because I enjoy the taste, and the sport of the hunt."

"And that's why you work for the Shadow King?"

"Something like that. Like I said, it's better to be the predator than the prey, and the Shadow King keeps me on the right side of that equation."

"What's he like?" I asked. "How did he get to power?"

The rabbit eyed me up for a second, searching for a reason to shut me up. Finally, he let out a big sigh. "It was ugly for a long time after Epiales died. The demon Etsop kept control for a while, but then he abandoned us, too. The Shadow King found a totem that gave him incredible power, and he was able to destroy any that opposed him to assume control of this land. It's kill or be killed in the Nightmare Realm, and he's the apex predator." The rabbit glared at me. "You should rest your mouth. You'll need it if you hope to live beyond tomorrow."

"Thank you for the advice." I rolled onto the ground. "What is your name, rabbit?"

"I don't see how that's relevant."

"It's relevant to me. If you're going to feed me to the

Shadow King, then at least I should know the name of my captor."

There was a long moment of silence. "Canterbury."

"That's a nice name. Goodnight, Canterbury. To better days ahead."

"You're pretty optimistic for a prisoner."

"Yeah, I guess I am."

CHAPTER 27

RED

I didn't like being a god's errand girl, but if Rama was planning something underhanded, then I needed to find the key maker first. If Rama was on the level, then I needed his plan to succeed. Either way, it meant finding the key maker, getting him to duplicate a key, and keeping it safe until I could suss out the truth. It was with that intent that I made my way across the city toward Odin's mansion, high atop a different, but no less impressive hill on the horizon.

However, I would not go to the key maker blind. I had the address of an old acquaintance of his, and before I went to my destination, whether it was my doom or my salvation, I planned to stop off and learn more about this key maker, and the battle for control of the universe.

Aniza lived in a small townhouse at the center of the Celestial Realm, surrounded by chic restaurants and hip shops. Her home was neither. If anything, I would describe it as seedy, which was something I never thought I would say about the Celestial Realm. All the townhomes around it were perfectly manicured, even if quirky in their own right, but Aniza's house was falling apart. The shutters hung low, and the awning over the front door sank as if a boulder had crushed it.

I climbed up the waterlogged steps and knocked on the door carefully—it seemed like it was going to fall off its hinges. After several long seconds, the door opened. Even in old age, the gods looked radiant and beautiful, but Aniza was homely, her shoulders slumped and face sagging from the weight of gravity.

"I expected you days ago," she grouched, a snaggle tooth catching on one of her lip sores. "Luckily, I don't have much to do but wait these days."

"I'm very sorry about standing you up," I replied, "Something came up."

"It always does." She stepped aside. "Come in. Leave the weapon at the door."

I nodded and laid the brahmastra against the wall of her foyer. "Of course."

She plodded through the room toward the kitchen in the back. "I'm surprised you found me, truth be told, and I'm oh so interested in what you mean to ask me about Shaun."

"Shaun?" I asked, confused. "Is that the key maker's name?"

Aniza laughed. "He was never that to me. He was just Shaun."

I took out a pad of paper and wrote down the name. "That is helpful already, but how could you think I wouldn't find you? Your house is in the heart of the city."

"You would think that, wouldn't you? But it has been hidden from prying eyes for ages." Every inch of the walls was covered in runes. Some I recognized from Earth, a combination of Norse and Egyptian carvings, but others were completely foreign.

"It's old magic," she continued, watching me study the walls. "Before he disappeared, my Shaun warded this place to prevent people from finding me."

"Is that why your home is so dilapidated compared to your neighbors?"

She shot me a look. "Partially, but they have the benefit of magic. I don't, and it's hard to find contractors in the Celestial Realm, especially ones you can trust."

It dawned on me then, watching Aniza as we headed back into the living room to wait for the tea. "You're not a god."

"Bingo." She poured the tea and sat down. "My love left me with some charms to help around the house and slow my aging, but that has wavered over time." She scratched her head. "I'll bet that's how you've been able to find me. The wards are failing. I always knew it would happen, but thought I had more time."

"More time before what?" I said, mixing a cube of sugar into my tea.

"Before you came for the key to the Dark Planet."

I shook my head. "The key has been lost for ages. I come to find your love and have him make a second one."

Aniza smiled behind her teacup. "For a woman as confident as you seem, you really don't know much, do you?"

I took a sip of tea. It was bitter like coffee, but not as strong. "I'm sorry. I am only repeating what I have heard from Rama, and what he has heard from others."

She set her tea down and scoffed. "It would be him, wouldn't it? At least it's not Zeus."

"Zeus is dead."

This time, she laughed. "Oh, that is too funny. Who did the deed?"

"I did." I pulled out the golden dagger. "With this. Metal pure enough to kill a god, and to forge a new key."

"Do you know what evil you tempt, opening the door to the Dark Planet?" she said. "The gods hid it away for a reason."

"Because they are afraid of the power that rests on the other side of the door. Power we can use to save the universe."

"Or destroy it. Power can save, but all too often it corrupts. The Dark Planet is full of the gods' mistakes. Opening that door will allow them to pour back out into the universe. Are you prepared to deal with the consequences?"

I cocked my head. "Can I be honest with you?"

"I wish you would. For too long I have been alone, and before then I dealt with the gods, who didn't believe I mattered enough to tell me the truth."

"I don't care what lies behind the door. I only care about exacting vengeance on the one who wronged those I love."

"You would destroy the universe for petty vengeance?" Aniza threw back her head and laughed again. "That is too funny, too funny. Well, I do appreciate your honesty."

"Would you protect them?" I asked. "Given all the pain the gods have caused, would you save them from the vengeance that the Dark Planet could bring down on them?"

Aniza wrapped her hands around her cup, looking someplace far away. "This really is good tea."

"I agree. That does not answer my question."

"Not all questions deserve an answer." She shrugged, but also bit her lip. "I do not know where my beloved is, but

I know that he took solace with Odin and made him the secret keeper of his location."

"Why did he trust Odin, but not you?"

"I am not eternal. While he thought me special, he knew I had the same faults as other humans. Odin is as pure as a boy scout, or at least he was in the age my Shaun left."

"Odin has agreed to give us the location," I said. "But I wanted to speak with you first, so that I could come to your —to Shaun, as a friend."

"Are you a friend?" she asked slowly.

"I am not an enemy, and if he is a friend to me, then I will be the best he ever had."

Aniza touched her collarbone, and then slipped her hand inside her dress. When it emerged again, she held a pendant of a heart, ripped in half down the center. "When you see my Shaun, give him this, and tell him that you are a friend of mine in a world where I do not have many."

She handed me the necklace and I stared at it in my palm. "Are you sure that I am worthy?"

"No, I am sure you are not, but it seems like this will come to a head any way, no matter what I do, and I would rather the key rest with you than any other who seeks to claim it."

I stood up. "I will bring your love back to you."

She smiled at me. "That would be nice. I would like to see him one more time, before the end."

CHAPTER 28

NIMUE

By the time the last vendor left for the day, my eyes were glazed over, and every muscle ached with exhaustion. My legs were asleep from sitting still all afternoon and far into the evening.

"Well, I think we did good work today," Flirget said with a smile. "I'm very satisfied with our progress."

I rubbed my eyes. "Is it over now?"

She nodded. "Absolutely. Tomorrow we will transform this space into the perfect wedding venue and get you married. Aren't you excited?"

I pulled myself to my feet and groaned. "Excited isn't the appropriate word, I don't think."

"That makes sense. After all, when the wedding is over Hastur gets his turn, right?"

"Is that what you call torture?" I asked. I wanted so badly to filet her, but I couldn't simply take my revenge on her if I wanted to be her savior.

A small boy in a frilly collar trotted down the stairs. He handed a note to Flirget and then ran off, his pale white legs catching the moonlight.

Flirget eyed the paper. "It seems the dark lord requests an audience with you."

"Of course he does." I sighed loudly. "Until tomorrow."

"If you survive."

She walked off with a spring in her step. The woman clearly wanted my engagement to fail. If she didn't have to plan an event, then nothing could go wrong, and she wasn't at risk of being sent to the dungeon. It gave me slightly more sympathy for her, but that didn't mean she had to be such a jerk about it.

On my way to the residence, my mind raced with reasons that the King in Yellow could want to see me. He had agreed not to touch me until the wedding night, but perhaps he learned of my deception and was ready to dole out my punishment, agreement be damned.

With a deep sigh, I opened the door to the dark lord's keep. The room's oppressive darkness seemed to drain all of its heat. This was unlike the dark lord, as his room was often filled with neon flowers or floating lights.

The room stayed that way for a moment, clad in a shroud of night, until the chill of the air poked like needles into my skin. Finally, a light heat emanated from the center of the room, kissing lightly at first, before rising into a blinding light that forced me backwards lest it scald my flesh.

From that light a hideous scream erupted, like the twisted pain of a thousand lost souls. After a long, terrible moment, the light dimmed again along with the shrieks, and a singular voice remained whimpering inside of it.

"Nimue!" a shout echoed. I recognized it immediately as Cassandra. "Help!"

She hung in the air, her limbs splayed out unnaturally taut like she was being pulled by ropes in every direction.

"Hastur!" I screamed. "We had a deal! You aren't supposed to touch anyone until our wedding night"

"I have not touched her," Hastur said, his red eyes glowing from the darkness. "And I have not harmed her. Cassandra, tell my betrothed that I have honored my agreement."

"Yes, Cassandra," I echoed. "Tell me, has he hurt you?"

She shook her head and winced. "No, he called me here and then placed me like this, but he hasn't touched me." Her lips slid as she spoke. My skin had become even more ill-fitting on her in the heat of the light.

Hastur smirked. "I told you. I am nothing if not a gentleman."

He was nothing if not a monster. "Let her go."

He held up his hand. "In time. Before I must know where Elvira and Bethel vanished to in such a hurry. I know it was not on assignment for me because I ordered them to stay in the castle. What could they be doing for you that takes them away from our nuptials?"

I took another deep breath. *Time for a world-class lie.* "Elvira told me she wanted to get some carnivorous flowers from her home and brought Bethel to help collect them. I heard they could be tricky to transport."

"It seems like a lot of effort for some flowers. They could be of better use in the castle protecting you."

"I told them they needed to be here before the wedding for that very purpose, but I believe they can be spared before then. Your event coordinator, Flirget, has been quite on top of all the plans. I don't think they will be needed until it is time to dress me for the ceremony."

"I hope that is true, for Flirget's sake."

I glowered at him. "I have answered your question, now

answer mine." I pointed at Cassandra's hovering body. "Why is she here?"

"As a present for you."

"A present?"

"I cannot have my beloved going to her wedding looking like that. My gift to you on the eve of our nuptials is the return of your skin to you...but I have a problem, because I cannot touch Cassandra, or you, to perform this gift, without your approval."

"This is a trick."

"It might be, but that does not change the question I pose to you." He stared at me. All I could hear was Cassandra's whimpers. "Do you want your skin back or not?"

He is baiting me. If I made one exception to our agreement, then he could find a way to make a hundred more. He was clever; he knew how desperately I wanted my skin back.

My eyes bounced between Hastur and Cassandra before I spoke. "Will you give her skin back to her as well?"

"That is not part of my gift."

"Then I request it to be added, and that you not hurt her in the process."

Hastur growled. "Ripping skin from her body will not be a pleasant experience. I cannot help that."

"I do not believe that. You created princesses out of nothing and can bend the world to your will. If you wanted it, then it would be done. However, if you are not powerful enough to make this happen painlessly, then I don't want it."

Hastur's eyes narrowed. "I am powerful enough to do anything."

"Then this should be easy for you. If you can return

both our skins without causing us pain, I will allow you to proceed, but only then."

"I could take your potion away and force you to experience the pain of your affliction fully."

The black ichor potion nullified the constant pain needling at my exposed flesh and the thought of losing it made me shudder, but I stood strong. "I know that you could do that at any time. I am not so naïve to think I have the power in this relationship. However, at this moment, you have asked my blessing, which means you are a man of honor." *You absolutely are not.* "If that is true, then you cannot do this without my approval. So, my question to you is whether you want your bride to look like I do, or as beautiful as you know me to be?"

I didn't break my gaze with him. I was not some weak thing, like those he was used to forcing his will upon. I was a rightful queen and knew how to deal with despots.

"You have hit upon my vanity quite expertly. Very well." He snapped his fingers. "I will make you see just how pleasurable my divinity can be."

Hastur lifted his hands and I rose into the air, my arms and legs splayed. My eyes closed from an unseen hand, and I felt a pulse of pleasure flow through me. It overcame me, again and again and again, my muscles pulsating with rapturous joy. I screamed out, not in pain, but in ecstasy.

Something squeezed every inch of my flesh for a moment, pinched, and then relaxed. When it was done, Hastur dropped me to the ground, and I laid there convulsing. I opened my eyes eventually and looked at my body. I was covered once again in the cracked black and white skin that Baba had given me, glowing white and glorious, with a universe once again spinning on my chest.

Cassandra wore a skin I had never seen before, bright

yellow, accented with red around her eyes and fire cascading down her forehead in a glorious mane. It was a perfect moment, and while there was still a long way to go before claiming victory over the King in Yellow, for one moment I had won a victory for us both.

CHAPTER 29

ROSE

"Do you need any help?" I asked as I helped Maricel back to the kitchen. We were carrying a half dozen bags filled with groceries and special ingredients.

"No offense, Rose," she replied. "But I think you have a better chance of screwing up my cooking than making it any better."

"Well, offense taken, Maricel," I said playfully. "But you're totally right. I could burn water."

Maricel and I planned to mask the crystal within a brined pork that she had been marinating all day. It wasn't exactly what Kadlu told me to do, but it was as good a plan as I was going to get. The meal would be heavy and salt-forward, which would make the crunchy crystal less obvious. It had the added benefit of making people, especially Rama, sleepy, just in case the spores controlling him became angry while we were trying to expel them. Though, now that he wasn't a god, I was confident that I could take him.

Maricel opened the refrigerator and started to put away

food. "Just relax. It's a big night and you need to be fresh for it. I've been doing this for a long time. I'll be fine."

"If you insist," I said. "I'll leave you to it." I headed back up to my room and yelped when I found Rama laying on my bed, hands folded over his stomach, waiting for me.

"I heard you and Maricel come back from the store. I figured you would want to freshen up for dinner and thought we should talk."

"I know this is your house," I said, leaving the door open. "But while I'm a guest here, I would appreciate if you didn't come into my room without knocking."

"Oh, I did knock, but you weren't here, so you couldn't answer."

"Then it's polite to leave and wait for me to return."

He pressed his hands on the bed and stood. "I think we're way past formalities here, so I will get down to it. I'm not sure what you are planning, but can you please stop trying to corrupt my staff?"

I leaned against the doorframe. "Oh, you mean the woman you have employed against her will, that just happens to share the same blood as your ex-girlfriend? That's a level of creepy I couldn't imagine, even for you."

"It was good insurance, for a time, that she would not take action against me." He grabbed my hand. "Now, it seems she has found a new way to infiltrate my headspace."

"Let me go." I spoke even keeled and level-headed, as I allowed a blue flame to grow from my free hand. "You are not a god, and you do not have permission to touch me."

He sneered and dropped my hand. "You are playing a dangerous game."

"As are you." As I stared into his eyes, the thick black goop congealing behind his pupil stopped, and I swore it looked at me before continuing on its way. "And now that you are only a human, it's a game you can't possibly hope to win against me."

He smiled. "That is where you are wrong. I have already won. It's just that the game needs to play out, like chess. I can tell that you have made a false move, and in thirty-six moves I will have won. You, and every other that has ever come in conflict with me, will soon see the folly of their ways."

"You tried to kill me, Rama," I replied, closing the door. "As long as we're putting our cards on the table, then let's be honest with each other. Your target was Kadlu, but I was a necessary casualty. Isn't that why you are a human now?"

"It might be. Or because I let your girlfriend fall into enemy hands and did nothing to stop it. I'm not sure which did the deed, since they happened in concert with each other." Rama crossed his arms across his chest. "It's inconsequential at this point."

I clenched my jaw. "I thought the thing you hated most in the world was being a human. Why would you be so willing to return to that life?"

He rolled his shoulders, feigning boredom. "It was the only way to move the pawns into their correct positions. Another necessary casualty in the war of attrition."

I took a menacing step, and he moved with a casual gait back toward the bed. "And you believe that when this is all said and done, you will still be standing? You think that the gods will fall in line behind you, a human?" He shook his head. "No, I think that when it is all said and done, me being a human won't matter at all."

"I will stop you," I replied. "I've done it before, and I will do it again."

"You have saved multiple realms, which is respectable,

but you've never been in a game like this, not with a contender like me."

I smirked. "That's what they all think before they go down in a blaze. I thought you were more interesting than all this, but it seems you're just another wannabe despot hiding behind the shield of democracy."

"I will bring democracy to this whole universe." He wheeled on me, his breath hot with anger. "And when I am done, you will all beg me to rule over you, but I will have no pity for you. I will simply laugh while you murder each other, and the universe burns as it devolves into its natural order."

"And what is that?" I asked.

"Chaos," Rama replied. "The gods have tried to bring order to the universe. They have fought against chaos, but it is futile. They will all see soon."

"The gods are a lot of things, but the thing they care about most of all is self-preservation. They won't lay down and let you run roughshod over them."

"I'm counting on that." His watch beeped and he glanced at it, then headed towards the door. "Odin is on his way. You should change for dinner. After all, this might be the last time you see your girlfriend."

"You'll regret this," I said. "I guarantee it."

He chuckled, his hand on the doorknob. "In all the time you've known me, have I come across as the kind of person that regrets things?"

"No, but there's a first time for everything."

"We'll see about that."

CHAPTER 30

BETHEL

I hated field work. Carcosa was vile, but at least it was clean. The woods Issha sent us to were filled with critters. We weren't there for ten seconds before one crawled up my arm. I spun and shot a fireball, hitting a tree and setting it on fire. Elvira laughed uncontrollably.

"What's so funny?" I asked as I brushed myself off.

She wiggled her fingers. "If you really wanted to kill that bug, you should have shot these fingers off."

"A prank?" I growled. "That is not funny. I hate pranks."

"I'm sorry, but I couldn't resist. Your low tolerance for bugs is legendary."

I narrowed my eyes. "I did not know you to be such a practical joker. I hate it."

"And I'm sure there is much I hate about you." She rose and pulled her shoulders back. "Even after all these years, we know very little about each other."

"Perhaps we can rectify that. What is your favorite torture?"

"Oh god, that is such a banal question. What is your favorite book?"

I jerked my head straight. "Do you have time for such triviality as reading?"

"Books aren't trivial. They are everything. Each contains an entire world inside of them." Elvira muttered a spell and a hardcover book appeared in her hand. "Yet entirely portable."

"I never thought of it that way."

She took a few steps and the leaves crunched under her feet. "Plus, the good ones allow you to hallucinate an entirely new reality. A truly great author is very much like a drug dealer, except the trip they take you on is completely safe."

"Nothing is completely safe."

"Take it. I want you to have it."

I put my hand up. "I will pass. If I want to read a book, I can visit the library in the castle."

She hugged the book to her chest. "But this is my favorite story. If you don't like this one, then you won't love any book I have to offer you."

"Very well, then." I took the book and placed it inside my cloak, muttered a spell, and allowed it to disappear until I had need of it. Then I paused, flummoxed. "I wish I had something to share with you."

Elvira waved me off with her hand. "Don't worry about it. I'm sure you will think of something."

"Flowers. I think I like flowers. I have spent much of my free time, what little I have, trimming the bushes around the castle, and I keep a collection of dried, dead petals on my dresser."

"That sounds lovely."

"I will bring you one, when we return to the castle," I mused.

"I would like that."

I didn't know that we could have rich inner lives as Elvira suggested. I wondered what sort of things Cassandra, Delilah, or even Nimue enjoyed outside of the torturous parts of being a princess. Could they have more to them than simply being a hand of the dark lord?

"I think that's it over there," Elvira said, pointing to a gnarled, black, half-dead tree on the far end of a clearing. "Be careful where you step."

"You will not trick me again, Elvi—"

An enormous claw swung at me in the darkness. It belonged to a monster, ten feet tall, thick patches of hair mixed with bare, bald spots, with glowing green eyes and hideous fangs.

"Watch out!" Elvira said.

I was not worried, even though the beast was enormous.

"It's more startling than anything." I raised my hand in the air. "Sit!" The monster did not listen, but instead chose to roar in my face again. "This will get unpleasant if you do not obey."

"Do you need help?" Elvira asked, wringing her hands.

"Not in the slightest. Go and get your note. I will handle this." I snapped my fingers and the monster's mouth closed. It stared straight at me with its hypnotized eyes. "That's better. Now sit."

"Fascinating," Elvira said.

"All animals, big or small, want nothing more than to be told what to do by a strong voice." I snapped my fingers again and pointed to the ground. "Down."

The monster dropped its head to the ground and then the rest of its body. Elvira walked up to it. "Years in the dungeons have taught you well."

"I think I will call it Henry. Did you get the note?"

She held up a letter. "Exactly where she said it would be."

"Lovely," I replied. "Then let us go see Baba. I think I will bring our new friend, either as another pair of fists in our upcoming battle, or as a gesture of peace from one powerful witch to another."

"That sounds capital."

I snapped my fingers. "Come, Henry. We have work to do."

NIMUE

Once we were alone again, far from Hastur's gaze, Cassandra fell sobbing into my arms. I managed to bear her weight, though only just, as we shuffled into my suite and closed the door.

"Are you okay?" I laid her over a lounge. Despite the fire that fell from her head, there was no heat, and the flaming hair was cool to the touch.

She clenched her hands together and spoke through gritted teeth. "I feel violated."

"I admit that I don't like my dalliances with the King in Yellow any more than you, but I thought this was what you wanted? To be wondrous and beautiful again."

Cassandra sat up slowly, wincing, and took a long look at her hands, now glowing a bright yellow and fitted to her fingers. "It is everything I ever dreamed." Her words had a breathless quality. "I am even grander than when he made me the last time, but...his gruff tone and harsh words...I understood those. They were made by a petty man out for vengeance and pain above all others. The way he touched, tenderly, almost softly, like a gentle lover..." Her body tensed. "I never wanted to know that he could give pleasure instead of pain."

I stood resolute. "This is what men like him do, unmoor you the moment you have made up your mind about them."

My visage in the full-length mirror caught my attention. My neck was long and sleek, porcelain, with small fissures of black cut into the marble and pooling in the hollow crater of my chest where a purple nebula spun on its own, slower than the eye could perceive unless you stared closely. The stars that made up my own personal cluster flowed down my arms and legs, causing my extremities to twinkle like the night sky. For as brilliant as Baba had been at crafting my look, it paled in comparison to the King in Yellow. He was a right bastard, but brilliant at shaping beauty into his monsters.

"I want to kill him," Cassandra hissed.

"And we will, my sweet," I replied, running my fingers through her fiery hair. "You just need to be patient until tomorrow."

Tears made of red fire fell down her face. "I don't know if I can wait that long."

"You must. We are nothing alone, but together... Together we will bring the king's whole empire crashing to the ground. Be brave, Cassandra. Be patient. We are so close to the end."

"Okay." She choked back her tears that dripped on the carpet and upholstery. "Did I ever tell you what I chose to stand against him at the beginning?"

"No, you never did. I assumed you were simply sick of living under his thumb, or that you craved his power."

"I wanted nothing of his power." She shook her head bitterly. "I wanted my freedom. I wanted a simple life that I could do with as I pleased. I thought I found that with a boy back home. He was handsome and dashing in all the right ways, but my father denied him, desperate to send me to Has—the dark ruler."

"I thought he killed your family."

She nodded. "He did, ruthlessly, once we agreed to the marriage. The only saving grace was that my beloved escaped the purge. I could never be with him, but at least he would be safe in another kingdom."

"But he wasn't, was he?"

She mashed her lips together trying to contain the tears. "For a while he was. He took solace in Bethel's kingdom in the north, and then Elvira's in the west, but eventually, the King in Yellow caught up with him. The dark ruler felt a personal slight against my love, and when his troops finally caught him deep in the woods trying to escape into Delilah's kingdom, he brought him to me...and forced me to kill him."

I gasped. "How could he—"

"He tortured him in front of the whole court, telling me the only way it stopped was if I took my love's life. He took such glee in my suffering, and in my love's pain. I finally took mercy on the only man outside my father that I truly ever cared about, and I watched the life drain from his eyes. In that moment, I swore revenge on the King in Yellow."

"I am so sorry," I breathed.

"To see him tender...to have him force me into rapturous lust ...it is one violation too many."

I knelt next to her. "We will have vengeance upon the dark lord for what he has done to you—to everyone in this kingdom."

"Thank you for letting me get that off my chest. I know

we are not friends, but you are the best one I have had in this place."

"That," I said, putting a hand on her shoulder, "is pathetic."

"Oh, it absolutely is."

I squeezed her hands together in mine. "We have this, sister. Go rest. Tomorrow is a big day."

CHAPTER 32

RED

Odin's mansion towered over the skyline from a dozen miles away, but I was still not prepared for its sheer scope, up close. Its white facade rose dramatically and lit up the sky against the black of the stars that competed with it for brilliance.

A call box stood outside the gate, a tall black wrought iron one with an "O" and "F" branded in gold on its upper edges. I pressed the call box and a shrill voice called out.

"Who's there?"

"Gabri—" I realized they didn't care my name, or who I was, just who I represented. "—I am Rama's girl. Come for what he was promised."

"It's about time."

The callbox buzzed and the gate clicked open. I continued up the driveway lined with marigolds until I came to the enormous white house at the crest of the hill. The door opened as I took the steps, buttressed between two columns at either end of the porch, holding up a widow's walk. A tuxedo-ed mud golem stood in the ante-room offset from the door, waiting for me.

The golem brought me into a sitting room and gestured to a small bench by a large window, then disappeared through an oak door. The window looked down onto the entire Celestial Realm. In the distance, the Crystal Keep shimmered, backlighting the houses and shops of the downtown area, including the portal station where I found Rose.

I lost myself in the view until a tall woman in a luxurious evening gown came for me. Her arms were thick with work and time, but firm, and when she shook my hand, my body remembered the exchange for several seconds afterward.

"Thank you for gracing us with your presence. I'm Frigg, Odin's wife. I'm sorry my husband could not be here to greet you, but he has already made the trek to Rama's for dinner."

"Oh," I said. "Does that mean Chelle is not here?"

"The gorgon girl?" she asked. "No, I'm to bring her later, once I have given you the location of the key maker."

"May I see her? Chelle, I mean. We are old friends, and I would like to be sure she hasn't been harmed."

"Oh, she has been harmed. Do you not know how experimentation works?" Frigg stroked her chin. "What is that expression? 'You can't make an omelet without making a few eggs,' or something of the sort. She is fine, though, if not slightly worse for wear."

"Thank you for your assurances," I said flatly. "I would appreciate it if I could see her."

The key to getting help from a powerful being was to play their ego with one side of your mouth and prove your formidable nature with the other. Too much of either, or not enough, would cause disaster. It took a light touch, like cracking a safe.

"Very well," she replied. "As a courtesy to Rama, I will show you to her. It will give me a chance to tell you about our collection as we walk. But leave the brahmastra here. It is gaudy, and likely to nick something in my collection—or me—if I let you carry it freely."

I laid the brahmastra against the window. "Of course."

Frigg and Odin seemed to have pieces in their collection from every planet and era in the known universe. It was no wonder they kept a large house. It was more of a museum than anything else, with each item meticulously chosen and their details intimately known by the hostess.

"And this piece we received from Hepilus 8, right before the tragedy that doomed their planet." Frigg pointed to a metallic vase. It had been manipulated in a way that I had never seen before, like it had submitted to the will of an intelligent and deeply disturbed higher being.

"It's...beautiful," I said. "And this is the way to Chelle's room, correct?"

She nodded. "It's a roundabout way, but I thought you would appreciate these pieces."

"I'm really in quite a rush. Rama expects results, after all."

She turned to me. "And yet you waste your time seeing your friend, an insignificant cog in the machine of the universe."

That part wasn't true. I knew as well as anyone that Chelle was a catalyst, and whatever that meant, she was clearly more than a simple cog.

"We are all, every one of us, hypocrites, human and god alike. Wouldn't you agree?"

"Perhaps." Frigg's smile faded. "Very well, we will end this once in a lifetime tour of the most expensive collection of rare art in the universe, so you can see your mutt friend."

"Yes, thank you," I replied, ignoring the insult. "I appreciate it."

"You had better."

CHAPTER 33

ROSE

My fight with Rama close in my mind, I retired to my room to bathe and prepare for dinner, making sure to lock the door multiple times, and even sliding a chair under the handle to prevent anyone from disturbing me.

Thank the gods for the make-up which smoothed out the freckles and other imperfections that I found all over me. Rama had the good stuff, too. The 'mama's got to entertain royalty' stuff that went on like butter and worked with a minimum of effort. I wished that Maricel could help comb out my frizzy hair, but she needed to focus on dinner so I was on my own to regret not cutting my hair before leaving Earth. I managed to put it up in a braid and even accent it with several white flowers I picked from the cluster on the windowsill.

Rama provided a sparkling mint green dress for the evening. Its hue washed out my pale skin, but it was apparently Odin's favorite color, so I bit my tongue and wore it without another argument. The long gown hung loose over my waist and tight on my hips, but while I examined myself in the mirror, it fit itself and conformed to the curves of my body.

There was a knock on the door, and I called over my shoulder, "Busy."

"I thought you might need a zip," Rama said. "Not sure why these magical dresses don't zip themselves, but I happen to have two free hands and a couple minutes to kill."

I growled but couldn't deny he was right. The dress was perfect below the navel but sagged across my chest because I couldn't zip it up myself. I stomped to the door and removed the chair before unlocking it for him. "I know exactly why they do it. It's just another way to make sure women are helpless without a man."

"I don't think it's as dastardly as all that." Rama walked into the room. "Turn around."

I pulled my hair off of my shoulders and turned. I felt the heat of his breath on my neck as he grabbed the zipper and slid it up slowly over my back.

"You don't have to be so gentle."

He finished and traced his hand down to the small of my back. "My apologies. I forgot you are not the delicate flower you appear to be."

My skin bristled as I leapt from his touch and turned around. "I don't know where you get off touching me like that, but this isn't a movie. I'm not going to fall in love with you because you zipped up my dress."

He cringed. "Oh gods. Just the thought of that makes me want to gag. I was just trying to help. I'm sorry people hurt you so much, but we're not all out to get something from you."

I laughed. "That's funny, because you are the most self-ish, neediest, conniving person I've ever met."

He held up his hands. "I didn't come to fight, really. Can't we go back to before, when we were grudging allies, at least for one night?"

I thought about the man Kadlu told me Rama once was, full of kindness, heart, and grace, how he fought viciously for the things he believed in, back before his mission was corrupted by whatever parasite festered deep in his soul, and how much I would very much like to meet that man.

"I would like that, actually," I said with a smile. "I will try harder, if you will."

"Trying hard has never been my forte."

I rolled my eyes. "Not everything is an invitation to deliver a pithy comment."

"I would not care to live in a world where that is true."

"I'm not going to fight you anymore. This is too big a night."

Just get through tonight, Rose, and if all goes well, you'll see that person Kadlu loved, and with any luck, the one you love as well.

"On that, I could not agree with you more."

I held out my arms to my sides. "How do I look?"

He stroked his chin. "I think even the most discerning gods would have trouble denying your beauty right now. You clean up nicely. I can certainly see what Hypnos and Persephone saw in you."

"Why, Rama, that was almost charming."

Maricel's voice rang out from the first floor. "Master Rama, they are nearly here."

He stuck out his elbow. "Let's put on a hell of a show."

I slid my hand through the crook in his arm and took a deep breath. "Sounds like a plan."

CHAPTER 34

BETHEL

Baba's house was unassuming. Dilapidated, even. For such a powerful witch, it was a disarming fact that immediately raised my hackles. "This is a trap."

"Of course it's a trap," Elvira said. "The question is what type of trap, and if we can traverse it without taking physical harm."

"That is less clear." I gave Henry a scratch under his monstrous neck. "Be a dear and go test the path for Mommy."

Henry gave a slow nod and plodded toward the house. For the first few loping steps, the monster didn't trigger a trap, but then, a dozen or so paces from the door, a series of stakes shot up from the ground and stuck right through two of Henry's feet.

"Your pet is in pain," Elvira said. "So sad to see."

"Shake it off, Henry." I looked at Elvira. "At least we know what we're dealing with—a primitive weapon."

Henry cried out in pain, then pulled his foot from the stake and took another step. A pair of glowing green skulls appeared, shooting a net from their mouths that yanked Henry to the ground.

"Henry!" I shouted.

I started forward, but Elvira stopped me. "Don't go getting sentimental on me."

The door to the shack opened, and an old woman hobbled out hunched over a knobby cane.

"You poor dear. Did you wander here on your own?" Elvira pulled me behind a thick tree before Baba's eyes could find us. "These woods are no place for a beautiful creature like you."

I peeked out from behind the tree, just an inch, so I could take in what was happening. Baba stepped forward and placed her hand around the monster's muzzle. She closed her eyes and sang a melody I had never heard before. It sent shivers down my spine. When she was finished, Henry let out a roar, and then, bit by bit, he disappeared into flakes of green mist.

"It was smart sending your pet to discover my tricks," Baba said, moving in my direction. I slid back behind the tree. "If only grachas were native to these parts I might have believed this to be coincidence. Still, he will make a wonderful addition to my menagerie."

"I mean you no harm," I shouted. "The monster was a gift from one powerful witch to another."

Elvira pulled my arm. "What are you doing? You'll give away our position."

I snapped my neck to her. "Isn't that the point? Wasn't our intention to meet with Baba and get her help?"

"Help?" Baba said. "That is funny, coming from a pawn of one who wants me dead."

It was a stupid idea, but I moved out from behind the tree anyway. "I do not come as an agent of the dark ruler."

Her lip twitched. "And who do you come from, then?"

"His intended queen, Nimue, as her emissary. She told me once that you two struck a deal, and I come to help her honor it."

The twitch of her lip turned into a smile. "You come to deliver me my crown?"

"We come with a message from your sister, Issha." Elvira joined me, holding out the letter. "If you have any love for her, you will read this. It will explain everything."

Baba's smile faded and her eyes narrowed. "I find that very hard to believe, Elvira, but I take solace in the fact that if you are lying, then I will have the pleasure of gutting you both for having the audacity to speak my sister's name."

"It has been a long time since I have been around one not afraid of me," Elvira said.

Baba took the letter and answered, "I do not fear you."

Elvira cocked her head. "We both know that is not true. We are smart, and so we should fear each other. The fact that you have no fear of us shows a lack of intelligence."

Baba chuckled. "I think that Hastur might have scooped out your brain when he made you, my dear." I bristled at the sound of the king's name, which made the witch laugh louder. "You have nothing to fear from him now. His magic does not carry into these woods. It might be the one place on all this planet where you are truly safe, from him at least. I, however, am another story."

Baba broke the black wax seal that bound the letter. When she did, a wisp of red flecks flew into the air. She smiled at that differently than she did at our insults, with an almost childlike sense of wonder.

"Do you recognize the magic?" Elvira asked.

She nodded. "It is my sister's, assuredly, and this was her seal. I have not seen it in"—she paused and appeared to swallow the emotion struggling to break through—"this does not prove anything. Magic can be forged, especially from one as powerful as Hastur."

Baba slowly unfolded the letter, and spent a long time reading it, her face contorting as she studied the words. Finally, she let out a deflated sigh.

"Do you believe us now?" I asked.

"Come inside," she said, turning to the door. "We have much to discuss."

"That doesn't answer my question."

"No," she replied. "It doesn't."

She pressed her hands toward the ground. When she did, the spikes that surrounded her yard withdrew, leaving unfettered access to her house.

"I have a bad feeling about this," Elvira muttered.

"You're only just now having bad feelings?"

"Should we continue?"

I nodded. "I believe so. After all, what is the worst that happens? We die? If that is our fate, at least it will be the end of all this."

Baba turned back. "Oh, death is the least of your concerns where you're going."

CHAPTER 35

ARIEL

When the rabbit Canterbury roused me again, I was surprised that I had slept, more so that I dreamed. My soul hadn't passed through the membrane of the Dream Realm, but in the haze of my waking I remembered floating in the Heart of Urgu, just for a moment. It was a wonderful hallucination before I crashed back into Sprig, and reality along with it.

"Hey!" Canterbury shouted, his face pushed close to mine. "Get up! We're moving."

I blinked at him several times. "Can I get a moment to—"

"No!" Then Canterbury snapped at the Seeker. "Bind her up tight and don't let her fall asleep again."

I shouldn't even have needed rest. I didn't in the Dream Realm, and yet, the further I walked from the portal, the more drained I felt. My feet were as heavy as my head, and I had to work not to drag them.

The rabbit glared over his shoulder. "Can't you walk any faster?"

When I shook my head no, he forced the Seeker to carry

me so that they could make better time. Eventually he hopped up onto its thin shoulder as well. The Seeker's long strides allowed us to cover distance quickly, and within two hours we had reached a small town filled with monsters like Canterbury—along with other twisted versions of cats, dogs, and other once lovely animals.

"We need to make final preparations for ascending to the castle. The Shadow King doesn't allow just anyone to travel to meet him, after all." Canterbury stopped in front of a pub and turned back to the Seeker. He parted a thick tuft of hair on his chest, revealing a jagged scar on his pink flesh, and said, "Away."

The Seeker touched its hand to the rabbit's bare skin. Immediately, the Seeker stretched and twisted in the air, then was sucked into Canterbury's body. When it had vanished completely, Canterbury steadied himself against a loose barrel.

"Hurts every time."

"What just happened?"

"The Seeker is bound to my soul." The rabbit shook his head. "No, that's not right. It is my soul, the worst parts of it. That is why it listens to my commands."

I looked around at all the animals walking the streets, each giving me the side eye as they went about their business. "Are all of these animals like you?"

He looked around and sighed. "It's not a pleasant life, but it's better than what we had to look forward to in the old days. The Shadow King keeps us fed, and the Seekers keep us safe. Nobody would ever be dumb enough to make trouble with us now."

I thought about the fact that Corben and I were ready to walk straight into the castle, and what a dumb idea that would have been, given what Canterbury just told me. It was good we were separated, and I had been taken, for we never would have made it to the castle ourselves.

The rabbit grabbed my rope and pulled me through town. When we finally stopped, it was at a large wooden building with two onyx-faced guards. They looked like the Seekers, except instead of being stretched longer than normal, they are squished down into short, powerful bodies extending horizontally to unnatural widths.

"Prisoner," Canterbury said. "I need to talk to Judith."

The guards did not say anything, nor did they prevent us from entering the building. Inside was a long desk that blocked any from moving past it. A bear with one eye hanging out of its skull turned its good eye to us as we entered. A collection of weapons and armor stretched back to the far wall.

"What do you want, rabbit?"

"I got a live one this time," Canterbury answered.

"You have said that before." The bear thought for a moment. "In fact, I believe the Shadow King gave you an ultimatum last time you came back with less than stellar results, did he not?"

"He did at that, Judith." My captor spoke in a fragile tone I hadn't heard him use before. "Which is why he's going to love what I have for him this time. I present to you Ariel of the Dream Realm."

Judith grunted. "Heard that before."

"Just smell her."

"Please don't smell me," I asked as pleasantly as I could muster.

Canterbury yanked me so hard I slammed my head on the table, which reminded me in no uncertain terms that I was a prisoner, and no more. The bear sniffed me slightly. Soon she was snorting voraciously.

"This is very good, Canterbury." Judith rose to her full height, smiling. "You might even make it back to even with the Shadow King after this."

A glimpse of a smile passed over his face. "You really think so?"

"No, but you might keep your head off the chopping block." The bear held out a slip to Canterbury, who loosened my rope. "Show this to the guard and they'll put her on the next transport."

Canterbury shook his head. "That won't work. I need to be there to present her. I want him to know it's me."

"You know what happened last time."

"I know, but if I don't do this, then I'll be looking over my shoulder every day of my life. Please, show some mercy."

The bear growled and ripped the paper from Canterbury's hand. She scrawled something on it and handed it back to him. "I don't know why I take pity on you."

Canterbury smiled. "Because you know how pathetic I am?"

"That might be true, but it's not something to be happy about."

"I'm just trying to get from the beginning of the day to the end. I'll take any help I can get, for any reason."

The bear waved him off. "Just go, and don't screw this up."

"I won't," Canterbury replied, pulling me to the door. "You can count on that."

CHAPTER 36

ROSE

Odin's carriage pulled up the hill toward Rama's house, and my heart dropped into my stomach when he exited the carriage by himself, without Chelle. I wheeled on Rama.

"You said he would bring Chelle," I hissed.

He held up his hands, but the placating gesture only infuriated me. I was ready to light Odin on fire.

"This is a power move. It's meant to rile you up and take you off your game."

I huffed. "It's working."

"We have the home field advantage right now. He has taken himself from his castle on the mount to dine at my humble mansion. He needs to unbalance us, and he has mercifully few leverage points. This is one of them." Rama sighed. "I had hoped it would not come to this, but I would be lying if I didn't think it was a possibility."

"I'm going to Odin's mansion and rescuing Chelle right now." I set my jaw and pushed past him, but he grabbed my arm.

"If you do that, then he will have won. We do not know what game he is playing, but we need him on our side."

"No, you need him on *your* side." I tried to wriggle free, but he held fast. "I'm on Chelle's side, that's all I care about."

Rama pulled me closer. "Then know this. He is smarter than you, and craftier. If you go trying to save your love, all it will do is doom her. Now, stop acting like a child."

With one final yank I pulled myself free. I studied his face for a moment, and while the black blobs darting across his eyes were disturbing, I saw desperation on his face, and realized something.

"You need me here, don't you?" I said, my eyes narrowing. "Whatever you have planned...you need my help."

He blinked, and then his eyes lowered. "Yes."

I raised my eyebrows and flashed a gloating smile. "And what do you need from me?"

"For a long time, Odin has coveted the Dream Realm. There are few places in the cosmos that the Board cannot touch, and it is one of them. He knows you are the one who permeated the Veil for the first time in a century. He knows you have Hypnos's blessing. He wants the Dream Realm. That is his price for helping us."

I scoffed. "You must be out of your damn mind. I'm never going to agree to that."

A knock on the door interrupted us. Rama turned, resting his hand on the door. "Then your girlfriend will die."

"She's my fiancée," I corrected him. "And if you insist on making me choose, I choose both every time."

"Sometimes I forget how naïve you are. You can't have both. You're not a school child."

He didn't give me the chance to snap back at him but opened the door. The old, snaggy-haired Odin, wearing a long coat and a patch over one eye, loomed in the doorway.

I wanted to boil him alive right then and there, but I feared that Rama was right, and Chelle was guarded by a powerful enemy. I couldn't let slip that I was having second thoughts until she was safe in my arms again. My etiquette lessons flooded back to me, and I straightened my back and put on my biggest smile.

"Odin, my friend," Rama said, giving the god a firm handshake. "It's so good to see you. May I take your coat?"

"You, personally?" Odin grunted. "I must be important if a god such as yourself would humble himself to such a menial task."

Rama bowed his head. "Tonight, you are the most important god in the universe."

Odin patted Rama on the shoulder. "Every day, my friend, that is true, but I will forgive the slight."

He slid off his coat to reveal his perfectly tailored, pin-striped suit. He shook his hair free, and it fell perfectly to his shoulders.

"I'll be right back," Rama said, gesturing with the coat in his hands. "Meanwhile, make yourself at home."

Odin made eyes at me. "And you must be Rose, the Dreamer. The whole of the Celestial Realm is abuzz with what you have done for the gods. Saving the Dream Realm, rescuing the Underworld, raising the Sunken Kingdom. You have done more in your short years than most gods do in an eternity."

I curtsied. "Thank you. I never know what to say when people give me a compliment, but I am very appreciative of your kind words."

He reached forward and kissed my outstretched hand. "So humble. It's refreshing given the gods I usually meet with."

I bent my head low. "It is an honor to be in your presence. Please, give me word of my beloved, Chelle. She is in your care now, I hear."

He dropped my hand and furrowed his brow. "Yes, she certainly is. You consort with fascinating creatures."

"She is not a creature," I said with a flash of anger. "She is my love."

"Of course. I meant no offense. It's just...to be made of pure magic is not normal. It's expressly forbidden, in fact. And yet, you seem to pass your time with two such beings."

My muscles clenched in panic. Red. "They are my dearest friends, and closest confidants. If anything were to happen to them, then—"

"Perish the thought," Odin said, waving his hand. "Your love is right as rain. In fact, my wife is preparing to bring her to you as we speak. All she needs is the word from me."

I exhaled. "That is good news."

Rama clapped his hands lightly from the doorway. "I hope you are hungry, Odin, for we have a feast prepared for you."

"I'm famished." Odin leaned towards me and spoke with a faux whisper, "Experimentation takes a lot out of me."

I pursed my lips and held my hand out to the door. "Then please, follow me into the banquet room."

CHAPTER 37
BETHEL

I gave Baba the benefit of the doubt that the inside of her shack was nicer than the outside, or at least bigger, but she'd used no magical spells to elongate the interior or gussy it up in any way. All I found inside its walls were protection charms and defensive wards. They were faint, and old, carved into the fabric of reality itself, so that even if the house fell, the wards would remain.

"I haven't seen this kind of work anywhere outside of Hastur's castle." Saying the name sent a shiver down my spine. I hadn't spoken it in so long that I expected him to appear, but after ten merciless ticks of my internal clock, he did not appear, and I let out a sigh of relief.

"I told you not to worry about saying the name," Baba said, watching me. "Though don't get too comfortable doing so, as the protections only extend to my home and the immediate area around it."

"I have no interest in staying here any longer than necessary," Elvira said. "Now, you said we had much to talk about. Would you care to elaborate?"

Baba walked to a small stove and turned on a tarnished

kettle. "I would not, but it seems that I have no other choice, under the circumstances." She placed the letter on the rickety table in the center of the room. "Do you know what is contained inside this letter?"

"No," I replied, walking to a ratty chair by the old table. "You can tell the magical seal wasn't broken before you cracked it."

"I thought maybe my sister would have explained it, given what she expects of you." She finished boiling the water and poured three cups. "Though, that is very much like her."

"No tea for me, please," Elvira said. "I try not to accept things from odd women who live in rickety shacks in foreboding woods."

"This is a special tea." Baba reached into a tilted cabinet above the stove and pulled out a rusted tin. Inside, she pulled out a collection of dead leaves, roots, and mushrooms that turned even my usually steady stomach. "You will need to drink every drop if you hope to traverse my prison."

"Your prison?" I asked. "What do you mean?"

Baba smiled as she placed the concoction into porous black pouches and placed them into the cups. Then she brought them over to us.

"She really didn't tell you." She set down a cup for Elvira, who took a seat next to it, and then left one in front of me before sitting down across from us. "How much do you know about Hastur, and the origins of his birth?"

I thought for a moment. "When the gods came, they needed a ruler for this place, and so they brought their chosen son to lead the dark planet and keep it in line."

Baba chuckled. "That is quite the story. I admit, I have not disputed it until now, for it was unimportant to deposing him, but the truth is much more twisted than that."

"And what is the truth?"

The old woman looked both of us in the eyes as she continued, "The truth is that this planet was once beautiful and bright, full of the kindest and gentlest creatures in the universe, but the gods needed somewhere to imprison the horrors they could not bring themselves to face. They chose this planet and cast us into darkness. The people of this planet did not take kindly to that and fought back with everything they had.

"They almost succeeded in bringing our planet back from the brink. The gods could have stayed on this planet to keep us in line, but none of them wanted that responsibility. And so the wickedness of the beasts they left us only worsened."

"Then how—"

She held up her hand to stay my question. "This is hard enough for me to get through without you interrupting." She took a long drink of her tea. When I didn't protest, she continued. "My sister and I were old even before the world turned, and we were hungry for power. We had been cast out by the monarchs who ran this planet, and we were bitter. The gods knew of our power, having blessed us themselves. They offered us the ability to unleash our wickedness on those who wronged us and so we conjured a being of such malice that it would burn the planet to the ground to keep it in line."

"Hastur," Elvira said, shocked.

Baba nodded. "We demanded the blood of a god for our work, and they agreed, so long as we never took up arms against them. They bestowed us great power, but their true strength was reserved for the creation we were planning.

The power of a god flows through his veins, but with none of their virtue, he quickly turned against us. We begged the gods for help, but they left us. I had placed a failsafe into the king of Carcosa, but I could not get close enough to use it. That is why I brought your future queen here, to do what I could not."

She slammed her hand on the table. "But now I found out my sister worked against me. She knew of my failsafe and created one of her own to overpower mine. Issha was always prouder of Hastur than I was and stayed by his side until he slaughtered her. Only in death did she see the error of her ways."

"The locket," I said, holding the sides of my tea. "The one that has Hastur's heart bound inside of it."

The old crone nodded. "She buried it deep in my prison, as a final twist in my side, and hid this letter to show me how to retrieve it should she ever die." Baba held up the letter and read:

Dearest sister, we have made a terrible mistake. You tried to warn me, but I was blind to power, and lustful for more. Now, I know that I was wrong. I am going to try to end this, but if it does not work, there is one more thing to try. I have hidden a locket inside of your prison...not the me of today, mind you, but a foolish child who thought she knew better than you. It contains all that remains of Hastur's cold, dark heart. If I am to die, please retrieve the locket, combine the locket with our horrible son, and end his life like you had always planned. It will only take touching the locket to his body to combine them together once again. I wish I had such clarity as I do now when you still spoke to me. Love, your Issha.

Baba cleared her throat. "On the back is a map to the location of the locket, written in my sister's blood."

"She must have tried to kill Hastur and failed."

"That is what it sounds like, but it does not matter how she died. All that matters is that we do what must be done. Now, drink. You must if you are to traverse the prison below. It will fortify your senses so that the madness does not catch you."

"Us?" Elvira said. "Why not you?"

She smiled. "I have long since given up on the world."

"That's a lie!" I shouted. "You sent Nimue to kill the King in Yellow just days ago."

"I have made my decision." Baba dropped her head. "That is how it must be. Either you two enter, or nobody does. Now, drink your tea."

"And if we refuse?" I asked.

"Then you already know what will happen. Nothing. The world will keep turning just as it has for thousands of years."

I grabbed my cup and began to drink. Elvira looked over at me. "What are you doing? What if it's poison?"

"Then let it kill me. I would prefer it to this life."

But it did not kill me. Instead, a sense of calm wrapped around me, and it was as if my eyes could see for the first time in my long life. I saw Baba not as an old woman, but as a brilliant collection of light glowing in a hundred different colors. Behind her, a door opened that led down deep underground.

I smiled at Elvira. "Are you coming, sister?"

She was still for a moment then, finally, lifted the tea to her lips.

CHAPTER 38

ARIEL

Canterbury and I waited at the base of the mountain for a transport up to the castle. There were hundreds of twisted animals, their prisoners, and shadow guards of all shapes and varieties who prevented any from continuing up the mountain pass.

Eventually, a wagon made its way down the mountain and offloaded its cargo: several monstrous animals, a dozen barrels, and a cache of weapons. When it was empty, the cart turned around and stopped. The guards pointed to a mangey basset hound who pulled three red-headed children along, a hunched elk with broken horns with a barrel-chested man as a prisoner, and Canterbury.

"Let's go," the rabbit said, pulling me forward.

We made our way onto the cart without a word and sat across from each other as the gaunt horses made their way without a driver back up the mountain. I was glad for it, as I barely had the energy to continue. I felt Hypnos's blessing draining from me.

Every hundred feet or so, a new pair of guards eyed us to make sure we weren't up to any funny business, but I wasn't planning on doing anything drastic. This was exactly where I belonged. Now, I just needed a plan, and somehow, I believed that would come from Canterbury, if he would open up to me.

"What happened to you last time you saw the Shadow King?" I asked after we were halfway up the mountain. Even the other mangled animals wouldn't look at Canterbury.

"I don't want to talk about it," he said hoarsely.

"I don't much want to talk, either," I said. "But I find myself feeling sorry for you, my captor, so I thought I would ask. If you don't want to tell me, that's okay."

There was a long silence where the rabbit looked out onto the horizon, and then, his eyes trailed over to me. "I used to be one of the Shadow King's prized Seekers, you know. If there was an impossible object, or person to track, he would give that assignment to me." He pursed his lips. "I must have increased his power ten-fold, but there was a little girl...she was powerful—the kind of magic you only see once in a lifetime if you're lucky. She could rival the king's power, and that made her a threat." He swallowed. "I tracked her down for him. We slaughtered everyone she cared about, and I brought her back to the king."

He bit his lip so hard it started to bleed. "Even after all I did to her, she didn't hate me. She was kind to me when nobody was, and I lost my head. When the king went to kill her, I stopped him. It was stupid, and it didn't matter much, as he flung me away with barely a thought. She died all the same, and the Shadow King lost all confidence in me. It was only because of my long history of service that he didn't slaughter me right there. Instead, he told me not to come back without a way to open the portal to the Dream Realm. If I did, he would dust me."

"Me," I said. "You think I can open a portal to the Dream Realm."

Canterbury nodded. "I thought it was a fool's errand until I saw that portal open and found you. It's a silly thing, but you are my salvation."

I leaned forward. "I don't blame you. I know I should, maybe, but I don't. After all, you led me here, which is exactly where I need to be to find Rapunzel's eye."

He looked at me for a long time. "You really do want to meet the Shadow King, don't you? You have no fear of him?"

I shrugged. "Should I?"

Everyone else in the wagon gave a solemn nod in unison, including Canterbury. "Everyone else does."

"I have already died once, and I should have died many more times in my long life. This is all bonus time for me. Bonus time most people don't get. So, I will make the most of it for as long as I am able and do so with as little fear as I can muster."

Then something happened I didn't expect. Canterbury spoke slowly and softly, checking after every word to see if he was being watched before continuing. "If you do somehow manage to survive meeting him...then he keeps the eye on a staff that allows him to harness his magic."

"An eye?" I asked, with the same hesitation and caution. "Are you sure?"

He leaned towards me, his tone and movement connoting confidence in the secrecy of our palaver. "Absolutely."

"How do you know that?" I asked, untensing my shoulders slightly.

"Before he was the Shadow King, he was Kelvin." Canterbury glanced around. "A frightened man who thought everything was out to kill him. He was right, of course, but the fear consumed him. During that time, he had just one single friend in the world."

It clicked into place. "You."

He nodded. "I was not always this twisted thing, though I was never what you would call adorable. When we found the eye deep in the caverns of Sprig, we thought it a boon. It meant we could fight back against everything that tried to kill us. He discovered the Seeker inside of me in those first days, and that he could raise an army out of the darkness to consume this land. It was not long, though, before that power consumed him."

"Why are you helping me?" I asked.

"For one, I am very sure that it's useless to tell you," he replied. "For another, though...I miss Kelvin. Most days, I just want my friend back."

I rested my hand on his. "Maybe there is hope for him still."

"No. There is no hope for him, and there is no hope for you, either. You're just too dumb to realize it."

CHAPTER 39

RED

The precious sculptures and priceless artifacts thinned out as we approached a long, plain hallway. It didn't seem possible that the bland walls could be part of the same house as the one that we had been walking through, full of ancient tomes and carved wood, and yet, Frigg kept walking as if the decor hadn't transitioned completely and it was as normal as breathing.

"Here she is," Frigg said when we finally came to a steel door.

Chelle sat inside a small cell. She looked as if she dropped more than two stone in the days since I had seen her. Her cheeks were gaunt, and skin hung loosely from her bones.

"What have you done with her?" I asked.

"She's fine." Frigg turned from the door. "Now, if we could cont—"

"I need to examine her to make sure she is not hurt," I replied, gesturing to Chelle. "Open the door."

"You asked to see her, and I obliged," Frigg replied. "You see with your eyes, not your mouth or your hands."

"I need to be assured she is okay," I said. "You still have something I need, if you remember, so there is no incentive for me to deceive you."

Frigg's face pinched. "You are toeing a very dangerous line."

"I know that, and yet, I will gladly cross that line for my friend. How far will you go to prevent me from seeing her?"

"And if I let you examine your friend, will you be satisfied?"

"Absolutely not." I stepped forward. "What I want is for her to be set free, but what I asked for is simply to make sure she is okay, because that is a reasonable request."

Frigg stared me down and then finally said, through gritted teeth, "You will have two minutes, and then we will conclude our business, as I have other more pressing concerns to deal with tonight."

She pulled a green key out of her pocket and used it to open the door. I stumbled inside the moment there was enough room for me to enter, and Chelle skittered to the wall.

"Get away from me, demon!" she shouted.

"No, Chelle, it's okay. It's me, Gabrielle, your friend. Do you remember me?"

Her eyes were wide and crazed. "I don't know what kind of trick this is, but you are not my friend."

"What have they done to you?" I asked. There was only one thing that could get her to listen. "Rose sends her love."

She leapt on me and clawed at my face. "You lie! Don't you dare use her name!"

I spun her over and grabbed her arms, slamming them to the ground easily. She was weaker than I had ever seen her. "Listen to me, Chelle. Rose is coming for you, okay? She loves you. You don't want her to see you like this, do you?"

She blinked and for a moment I could see my friend behind those wounded eyes. "Red?"

I nodded. "Yes, it's me. I promise. Remember when we met on the road in the underworld, and we saved the world together from Zabasha?"

"Zabasha…" Her face softened. "Red. It really is you, isn't it?"

She wrapped her arms around me. For a moment I thought that she was going to attack, but as she held me close, I realized she was weeping.

"It's okay," I said. "It's going to be okay."

"Why does this always happen to me?" Chelle whispered. "Am I a bad person?"

"No, you're not. The world is not fair, and it is least fair to you."

"Time!" Frigg barked.

I pulled Chelle closely and whispered. "In my belt there is a golden dagger that can kill a god. Do you remember when I used it on Epiales?"

She wiped her eyes and nodded. "Yes, I think so."

"When I let go of you, I will turn, only for a moment, to block Frigg's gaze. When I do, you must take the knife from my left hip. If you fail, we will both be killed, or worse. Do you understand?"

She nodded again, and I released her. I pulled my cape casually to the left to prevent Frigg seeing what was happening. When I did, Chelle grabbed the golden dagger from my belt. I replaced it with another blade from the sheath on my wrist and then turned back to Frigg. Chelle scrambled back to her bed and slid the dagger under her mattress, following my shadow as I made the way to the door to conceal her.

"Are you satisfied?" Frigg asked as I exited the cell.

"No," I replied. "Whatever you have done to her is horrible, and I will have justice for her in time. For now, I believe she is safe enough, and will deliver this message to Rama and Rose when I see them."

"Hopefully she will be out of my care before then." Frigg led the way back to the warmth of the mansion. "Now, let us get you the location of the key maker, so that we can get you out of my hair."

CHAPTER 40

NIMUE

I woke up the morning of my wedding with less dread than I expected, considering this was the day I would either kill a king or be killed by one. I harbored no delusions that if I ended up married to Hastur, I would not survive whatever torture he had planned for me.

"Oh good, you're up," Flirget practically chirped, bounding into the room and pushing open the blinds. "I thought I would have to rouse you from a dead sleep. We have a big day ahead of us. Are you excited?"

I pulled the blanket closer to my face and grumbled, "You know I can kill you, right?"

She laughed. "You're not special in that regard. Now, you have breakfast with the princesses before your final fitting and lunch with the royal court. Then, we get you married. Oh, it's all very exciting."

I slid out of bed. "Are you always this perky, or are you just burning off nervous energy?"

She cocked her head from one side to the other. "I don't know what you mean."

I spoke slowly. "Well, if this doesn't go well, you're

going to die. I acknowledge that, and I feel bad about it. However, I'm wondering if you even care that if my marriage goes through, I'm going to die tonight."

She thought for a moment. "I hadn't really thought about it much, honestly."

I shook my head, every movement deliberate. "I don't believe that. You've been making snide comments since the moment we met, which is fine. I'm partial to them myself, but this might be the last quiet moment I get for my whole life, and you ruined it, so I have to ask, just how evil are you?"

Flirget smiled. "I don't think any of us are evil. We're just trying to get on any way we can. So, we swallow the pain and keep going."

"Right, numb yourself to the horrors." I was nose to nose with her now. "You've confirmed that you don't care even a little bit about the fact I will go to my death this day. It's troubling, but not unexpected. I didn't let the things I did as Queen of Oz sink in, either. Looking back, it kind of made me a psychopath. I wonder if it makes you the same."

"I'm sorry," she said. "But you did ask for this. As I hear it, you proposed to him."

I headed to my vanity. "We all do what we must to survive the present moment. I didn't think I would live for another hour if I didn't make a drastic choice. The ramifications of my proposal were future me's problem, which was fine then, but now it's current me's problem, and soon enough, we'll be at the end of this day, and that woman who kept pushing off her responsibilities will be tortured, and lucky to die before the end."

"It's—"

"Fine. It's fine. Can you leave me to get dressed?"

"Of course," she replied.

I opened my closet to find four different dresses, each more beautiful than the last. There was a red gown the color of blood, another as black as onyx that glistened like a polished stone, a blue dress that plumed at the back and the bottom, and a white dress, as pure as the driven snow.

"Which one is for breakfast?" I asked, unable to focus on the details of the day.

"The blue. We've cut each one so that the nebula turning on your chest shows on each one." She smiled, but there was also a pained expression that I hadn't seen before. "I want you to be happy, Nimue. You might not believe that, but it's true."

"Nobody has ever cared if I was happy in my whole life, so forgive me if I don't believe you."

Flirget shook her head. "That is very sad."

I took the dress from the closet and held it to my shoulders, checking the mirror to see how it would look. "Maybe you understand better than I gave you credit for."

She opened the door to my suite. "If you need anything, you can always holler out for me, and I'll come running."

"I need you to get me out of this whole mess," I said with a smile. "But that is impossible, so let's just try to get through it together."

She nodded silently and left the room.

CHAPTER 41

ROSE

We made it through the first two courses, a tomato bisque soup and an arugula salad with a mango chutney dressing, without blowing up on each other, mostly by speaking of nothing but small talk and pleasantries. Rama and Odin fell into the easy rapport so common among the rich and powerful. They had the same lived experience and knew the same people, so they mostly caught up about the news of the day, while I sat off to the side smiling and nodding, trying my best not to jam a knife through either of their temples.

"Nasty business with Zeus," Odin finally said after pushing the remains of his salad away from him. "How long had you orchestrated his demise, did you say?"

"Not long. It just came to me in a flash," Rama replied. "I find that it's best to have goals, but to let the plans be flexible based upon new information and allies. It wasn't until Gabrielle came to me with her golden dagger that I realized what could be done with it."

Odin took a sip from his honey mead, which he swirled first in its pewter, ruby-encrusted goblet. "It would have been nice to be made aware before the deed was done. I felt very much like I had egg on my face by allying with him when he was bound for death."

"It was a tenuous situation," Rama said, wiping the corner of his mouth with his napkin. "I could not tell any save for my most trusted inner circle for fear that it would go belly up. Even with the strictest of confidences, we nearly failed."

Odin looked up from his glass and his one remaining eye narrowed. "I would have thought I was in your inner circle. It hurts me that you don't find me trustworthy, given that you expect me to join the Board and tip it into your favor."

I had held my tongue for long enough. I was not interested in the machinations of the Board. I just wanted Chelle back. "Why should he trust you, when you experiment on his friends? It seems like you aren't as good as your word."

"Rose!" Rama smacked the table. "Quiet yourself."

Odin held up his hand. "It's okay, Rama. We have beaten around the bush long enough. I wondered when it would come to the heart of the matter." He turned to me. "I appreciate your bravado. Humans have historically cowered before me."

"You are not the first god I've met, or the most frightening. Two of your kind's blessings flow through my body, and I have met with countless others."

"You are certainly worthy, little human. Say what you need to say. I await your wise words."

"You talk in circles, but it seems to me that this all comes down to trust. You do not fully trust Rama, and we certainly don't trust you."

"She does not speak for me, Odin," Rama said. "I trust you."

Odin whipped around to stare Rama down. "Then you are a fool. Simply because I once stood against Zeus you trust that I would always stand against him, but I allied myself with him before his death, and turned on your gorgon friend to satisfy my own ends. I think your pet has the right idea. Trust no one."

"I am nobody's pet," I growled. "How dare you. I was queen of Oz and am the savior of the Fairy Realm. I bow to none."

"Those titles mean nothing to me, child." Odin's eye bounced between the two of us. "Do you know what your benefactor promised me to come here today?"

"He has informed me, but I assure you it was something he had no right to offer."

Before Odin could answer, Maricel stepped out of the kitchen holding three platters of pork chops. "The main course is served. I brined these pork chops myself this afternoon, and then fried them in a minced apple sauce, and serve them with spinach and mashed potatoes."

I was furious at Odin and desperate to know what Rama promised in order to get him to dinner, but it was clear that both of the gods at the table were against me in their way. I needed an ally, even if that meant poisoning Rama to get one.

Maricel slid a plate to Rama first, and then Odin, then finally to me with a wink. "Enjoy."

"Thank you, Maricel," Rama said, cutting through the pork chop. "It looks divine."

"It should," I replied. "It was made by a god."

"To our health," Odin said with a chuckle. "We will continue this after filling our bellies. Hopefully our animosity toward each other will lessen with our hunger subsided."

I moved the food around my plate, but I didn't eat anything from it. I was too busy watching Rama as he swallowed bite after bite. Maricel was a master chef. He didn't seem to notice the poison he stuffed down his gullet. But the crystals weren't working. Once he was done and had wiped his mouth, I knew something was wrong.

I hurried out of the room. "Excuse me."

Maricel was cleaning up in the kitchen and turned to me with a smile when I entered. "Something wrong?"

"Yes," I said. "What happened in there? The spores were supposed to be chased out of Rama by now."

She cocked her head and stuck her hand in her pocket. When she pulled it out, the blue crystal packet rested in her hand. "Oh this? I decided it would be better to infect you and Odin with our spores than to save Rama. After all, that would not further our ends."

I looked on in horror as a pair of black spores shot back and forth across Maricel's eyes.

"Don't fight it, dear," she cooed. "It will all be over soon."

CHAPTER 42

BETHEL

"It smells terrible down here," Elvira said, her voice funny from breathing through her mouth. "Like a disemboweled prisoner whimpering for salvation that will never come."

She wasn't wrong. When we reached the bottom of the stairwell, the stench of sulfur was nearly too intense to continue forward. I muttered a counter curse which blew the odor away and created a tight barrier around the two of us.

"I am surprised I don't like this place more," I said. The fog parted for us as we walked through it.

"I find it kind of cozy, save for the smell. I wouldn't vacation here, but it reminds me of home."

"Perhaps that is because Baba designed this place and designed the demon that now occupies the throne."

Strange mewling grew louder as we navigated to the location marked on the map. We turned one final corner and came face to face with the source of the moans. Cells stacked four high, separated by bone and sinew. The stone of the floor undulated beneath my boots.

"This I like," I said. "Perhaps I judged it too soon."

I had always thought that our dungeon was not nearly imposing enough. Yes, it bore all the traditional underpinnings of those castles I frequented in my youth, but that was precisely my point. There was nothing special about Carcosa's dungeons, save for those who doled out its punishment. It would have been so much more intimidating if our walls were made of muscle and skin, or our floors pulsated with untold terrors, even if it was only window dressing.

"It cuts an imposing image, doesn't it, sister?" Elvira asked. She smiled as she reached her hand out to one of the cages and the monstrous beast inside nipped at it. "These are war beasts with some teeth. I could see us riding these into battle."

I stood in the center of the room. "I haven't been in a good battle in ages, sister. I miss the days when kingdoms fell at our feet. Now that the royals have fallen in line, there are so few opportunities to bathe ourselves in the blood of our enemies."

Elvira turned to me. "Perhaps it is time to choose a noble to pit ourselves against, like the old days."

I cackled. "Do you remember Duke Ferdglig?"

She nodded. "He was so loyal, until we decided he was not, and the dark lord set forth to acquire his kingdom for our own."

"Those are the days I remember best, sister, cutting through the countryside, reaping the deaths of all we came upon, innocent or not." I sighed. "Do you think it is wrong to go against our king, who gave us so much?"

"And took so much from us, sister." Elvira's voice was a hiss. "Do you remember the look on your father's face before Lord Hastur ripped him in half?"

My voice trembled when I answered, "I will never forget

it, or the look on your poor mother's face before you slit her throat."

Elvira swallowed. "The dark lord has taken more than he has given, and our conspiracy is his justice come for him, just like it will come for us one day. None can rule forever. If you live by the sword, you will die by it."

I continued through the room, and when I got to the end of it, I heard a familiar yelp on my left. Henry was locked behind in one of the caverns, his head pressed against the bars.

"Henry!" I pet his head and scratched his chin. "Did she hurt you?"

"He looks fine to me," Elvira said. "Just like all the others."

I pulled on the bars, but they did not budge. "Perhaps we can get him out, if we—"

Elvira placed her hand on my shoulder. "This is not why we were here, and if we stop to help this poor animal, we might anger Baba."

"I don't care about that—"

Elvira slapped me across the face. "Don't be daft. I chose you because you are heartless, ruthless, like none other I have met. Grow a spine and say goodbye to this worthless mutt."

I snarled at her, but she was right. "I'm sorry for bringing you into this, Henry. Perhaps we will see each other in another life."

"You were the one that chose to use him as bait."

"I know, but seeing him here...I do not like it."

She pulled me away from the cell. "Perhaps we can convince Baba to let him out when this is done."

She was lying, but I still nodded and turned from him. Henry whined as we continued down the hallway, and my dark heart cracked slightly at the sound of it, only callusing back over once we were further away and I could no longer hear the cries.

"Do not break again," Elvira growled.

"I will not." As far as I could see, the cells continued. "How much further?"

Elvira studied the map. "If the scale of this map is to be believed, then quite a distance before we reach the end of this path, and then through the corridors beyond. Baba keeps quite a menagerie down here."

I surveyed our bleak surroundings. "She has been collecting for eons, everything that crossed her path. It must take an incredible amount of energy to maintain this prison."

The path finally led us into a cold and empty room, where the undulating underfoot did not follow. The cells were bitten through, the muscle and sinew gray and dead.

"This is not good."

I ran my fingers across the wall and found it gnawed, as if massive beasts had taken bites from the flesh of the prison. Then, a disturbing snarling sound grew closer.

"Prepare, sister," Elvira said.

A massive beast with glowing yellow eyes stepped through the shadows and swiped at my chest. Paper flecked off of my cloak as I staggered backward. I felt my chest, and pulled out Elvira's book, now slashed through with the beast's claw marks.

I tossed the book on the ground. "I'm sorry, sister. I very much looked forward to reading this."

"There are others, sister. Now, I think we must prepare for battle."

The beast snorted and smoke came from its nose, then fire shot from each nostril. On either side of it, smaller beasts half its size pressed forward and growled at us. Some had long snouts and others, tusks, but they all looked hungry.

"We mean you no harm," I said, holding my hands out.

"Speak for yourself," Elvira said with a shrug. "I mean to do battle today. All this talk of our previous conquests has me ready for a fight."

"Stand down!" I shouted to the beasts, but they did not stop moving. I stepped back and joined my sister as the monsters advanced. "I think you will have your chance. They do not answer to my commands."

"Good," she replied. "I lost out on hunting once today. I would be disappointed if I lost out on another!"

CHAPTER 43

RED

I followed Frigg back through the house, picking up the brahmastra on the way. She entered a large office festooned with wooden sculptures of birds of prey, where the walls were covered in bookshelves, and it smelled like leather and ink throughout the room. She pulled a sheet of parchment from the oak desk, placed a quill in ink, and began to write.

"Old fashioned," I said to her. "Nice."

"People are in such a hurry these days. Writing script forces us to slow down and appreciate our words, luxuriate over them, and make sure they are precise."

There was a question that I had been dying to ask her, and since our business was about to conclude, I couldn't hold it in any longer. "Why are you giving this to Rama? The secret of the key maker has been lost for an age, and yet, you give it to us freely."

Frigg laughed. "Not freely. Certainly not."

"Still."

Frigg blew on the ink to dry it after she finished writing. "Shaun is a stubborn old fool, and we grew tired of protecting him for little more than empty assurances that he would provide us with the key."

"Then you have met him before?" I asked.

"Met him, dined with him, watched movies with him. At every turn he assured us that he would make us a new key to the dark planet, but it never transpired. He always had one more request of us. We tire of it endlessly, so we welcome the chance to get rid of this pest. We were close to killing him ourselves."

"Rama made it seem like this was a closely guarded secret, and that his weapons were the only in the universe that could make a new key."

Frigg folded the letter and handed it to me. "He is arrogant, like all men. The metal in your brahmastra is rare, but the universe is vast. Any god with half a brain could find it if they looked."

"Rama never could."

Frigg arched an eyebrow. "My point stands."

"You don't think much of him, do you?"

She opened her mouth to speak but seemed to think better of herself. Her face fell. "We wouldn't have taken your friend if we thought highly of him."

"And yet, you work to ally yourself with him."

She smiled. "Our motives are our own, and excuse me if I don't wish to tell them to Rama's errand girl."

My jaw muscles clenched. "I am more than that."

"I don't care." Frigg began shuffling items on the desk. "That letter in your hand grants you permission to use the portals, which had better be all you need from me. Now, get out of my sight."

I had been around enough powerful people to know when I had overstayed my welcome, and when they were close to slitting my throat. Frigg was at the edge of her patience, and so I took my leave and made my way across the Celestial Realm. Now that I had the location, I felt the need to be swift, but I wanted to tell Aniza what I had learned.

Her house was even more rundown than the last time. The steps which creaked the last time I came to the house were now snapped in half. The door was ajar and so instead of knocking, I pushed it open slowly. Something was amiss.

I held the brahmastra tight. It was the only weapon I had against the gods, and while I would soon give it to the key maker, right now it was mine, and I would wield it against any evil that lurked here.

A woman laid dead on the living room floor, her blood seeping across the carpet. She was young, and even in death, her eyes still sparkled like the sun. She was a goddess, that was for sure, and that meant whoever killed her had a weapon infused with the same material as the brahmastra.

"Ah, Gabrielle," Aniza said, stepping into the room with a cup of tea in her hands. "It seems our last conversation brought with it some unintended consequences." She looked at the walls. "The wards have failed me. I hoped it was just a one-time occurrence with you getting through the barrier to find me, but I am not so lucky, it seems."

I looked around at the room. "You should come with me. I have the location of your beloved. I'm going to him right now. I came to tell you, but now I think you should come with me."

"Unfortunately, I think that is the wisest course of action." Aniza nodded and took another sip of her tea. "I look forward to seeing him again. I hope he remembers me."

"I don't think anyone could forget you, Aniza."

"Funny, because that's exactly what they have done for eons." She put down the tea. "Let me find a coat and a hat, and then we'll be off."

CHAPTER 44
NIMUE

"Ow," I said to the tailor as she pinned the dress to make her final alterations. "The dress is what you need to hem, not my leg."

"Sorry, miss—queen." Her hands shook. "I'm working the fastest I can to make it perfect for tonight."

Perfect. That was what everyone cared about, even if it came from pain.

"It's okay, Ciyl," I muttered. "I'm already bait. I might as well bleed too."

"I'm sorry, my queen?"

I simply smiled. "Nothing. You're doing a great job. Is this your first wedding?"

"Royal wedding? Yes. Wedding? No. I did a couple dresses for nobles last year. They were lovely about it. Their raving's what got Flirget to appoint me the royal seamstress." She was crying as she spoke and stopped pinning to wipe her mouth. "I'm sorry. I don't mean to be ungrateful. It's just—"

"I know, Ciyl," I said. "I know. We're all in the crosshairs today, so let's all do our best to be perfect, and we'll try to get out of it with our heads on our bodies."

"And if it's not perfect, my queen?"

I smiled. "Then we get to be done with all of this, and rest. Won't that be nice?"

She thought about it for a moment, and then her eyes brightened. "That sounds lovely. Much better than the getting my head lopped off part, but the resting part is nice."

"After tonight, I hope none of us have to deal with the head getting lopped off part ever again."

"Well, that would be lovely, too."

The door to my suite flung open. Hastur stood there, clad in a long flowing black and yellow robe adorned with sigils, glyphs, and runes that trailed him like the train of a dress.

"You're not supposed to see the bride!" I shouted, leaping back off the podium where Ciyl had placed me.

"Is that a rule where you come from? It's not one here." He turned to Ciyl. "The hem is uneven."

The poor girl nodded furiously. "I aim to fix it, sire."

"See that you do." He waved his hand dismissively. "Now leave. I need to speak to my betrothed."

"I'm really very busy," I replied as Ciyl hurried to pull the white gown off my body. "This is my wedding day, after all."

"This cannot wait."

Ciyl zipped my dress down and I stepped out of it before she sped out of the room, leaving me in a matching set of white, lace underwear with garters holding up knee high stockings. I planned to slide a knife inside them for good measure, just in case all our other plans failed.

"You look ravishing," Hastur said, but his tone was flat. "Perhaps I could get a taste of tonight early."

"No, I don't think so." I threw a black silk robe over my shoulders. "You said you had need to discuss something with me? Was it to compliment my body, or something actually important?"

"Elvira and Bethel were spotted in the woods near Cassandra's old town, and far from the north where you claim they were going."

I raised my eyebrows. "Interesting, and you are sure it was them?"

"My girls are nothing if not unique." He was watching me closely. "My informants are sure."

It was a wrinkle in my plan, but not wholly unexpected. I had certainly lied successfully over less conspicuous intel. I shrugged. "That is very disturbing. I'm sorry that they are where they shouldn't. I only know what they told me."

He growled. "Or you are lying for them, plotting something behind my back."

I laughed, half nervously and half to cover that laughter up. "Have you ever met your princesses, Hastur?" I hated his name on my tongue. "It's all I can do to get them in the same room without sniping at each other. You have them well-trained in that respect."

"I do not believe you," he barked, taking a menacing step forward.

"Do you believe anyone about anything?" I stared directly in his eyes, unflinching. "I am very powerful, but if you are claiming that I somehow got your princesses to work together in some complex plot against you...well, I would have to be the most powerful witch in the universe to work that kind of magic. Were you coming in here to give me such a compliment? Because if so, it's the greatest gift you could have ever given."

He raised his hand. "Watch yourself. I do not like your tone."

I placed my hands on my hips. "You can't touch me until the wedding, and I'm very sure that no matter what I do before then, it won't change my fate. I could bow down and praise you for the next few hours, and it would not stop me from being ground to oblivion under your boot after taking my vows."

"You are right about that."

"It's a shame, because if I were that powerful, I would be a very powerful ally. I could control your princesses where even you can't. I could be every bit your equal. Of course, that's a silly notion, since nobody could equal the great King in Yellow."

I was prodding him, like poking a cobra with a stick. If he turned his ire on me, it would be averting from Bethel and Elvira. With any luck they were with Baba right now, gathering the locket. I needed to give them all the time in the world.

"If I find out you are lying to me, I will kill you all and start again with new princesses. You are not so grand without my magic. Remember that."

I put up a finger. "That is where you are wrong. I have always been grand, and I will always be grand. With or without you. Now, leave. I must prepare for greeting our honored guests."

"You dare command me!"

I summoned my courage and squared my shoulders. "For today, I do. You can stuff your anger inside and take it out on me in a few hours, but until then, I am in charge." I opened the door. "Now, go."

He gave me a vicious look before spinning on his heels and heading towards the door, his robe trailing behind him. "You will live to regret this," he roared as he stomped off.

"I do hope so," I called after him. "Until the next we meet, husband."

CHAPTER 45

ARIEL

Over my long life I had seen a lot of castles, and they often took on the personality of their master. Given what I knew about Canterbury's friend Kelvin, the Shadow King, his castle was less twisted and gnarled than I thought it would be. If anything, it was a plain affair, with none of the flair I anticipated.

"Will you stay with me?" I asked Canterbury as we stepped off the wagon.

He nodded. "Until the Shadow King conveys his favor back on me."

The shadow guards led us across the threshold towards the castle. I felt the fear coming off the prisoners like the heat off a stove, but I was calm. This was exactly where I was supposed to be. Now, all I had to do was speak to the Shadow King, grab his staff, and escape the castle. From there, I would find a way back to the Dream Realm, and Urgu.

Simple, right?

"Hey," Canterbury said as we walked. "I really am sorry that you have to—well, whatever happens. I do feel raw about it. You weren't horrible, which is more I can say about most humans I've ever met.

I smiled, my eyes heavy with desire to sleep. "Thanks. While you are horrible, I'm sorry about what happened to you. If I could fix it, I would. I hope you know that."

"Yeah, but there's nothing you can do, is there?"

"There might be yet. It's not over until it's over."

"You're literally walking to your doom, and you're thinking positively. You must be the most upbeat person I ever met in all my years. Is that what the Dream Realm does to you? Fill you with hope?"

I shook my head. "I don't think so. There's dark and light everywhere, in different measures. I think how you feel depends on where you look, and how you look at it. If you look at the darkness and look for evil, that's what you'll see, but mushrooms thrive in the darkness. So do owls and some of my favorite pixies. And light can be joyous, but it also burns if you stare at it too long, and if you don't protect yourself, it'll burn you up."

Canterbury let out a low whistle. "That's the dumbest thing I ever heard."

I shrugged, weakly. "Maybe it is, but it's how I keep hope, all the way to the end."

"By gullible idiocy. Got it."

"By believing in the best in everything, even you."

"There ain't any good left in me, sister."

"There might be yet, little rabbit. Remember, we haven't reached the end of the story."

We stepped under an archway into the castle proper, and all the light died. We were bathed in darkness and clothed in the abyss.

"We're nearly there," Canterbury said. "I suspect they'll see you first, given what they know about you."

"Wonderful," I replied. "Then maybe I can save all these prisoners, too."

"Gotta hand it to you," Canterbury said. "I almost half believe you'll do it."

"Always believe, Canterbury. That's one thing I will keep with me, no matter the outcome. Always believe. I have forgotten that at times in my life, but the darkness has brought me back into the light."

CHAPTER 46

RED

Subterfuge and stealth were two of my greatest strengths, but they were not Aniza's. We stuck out like sore thumbs every time she was forced to hide from possible threats. Somebody was out for the key maker's wife, which meant we had to be careful to make sure nobody caught wind of her.

"Over here," I whispered when we finally arrived at the portal station. It had taken several hours to cross the city with our circuitous route, squatting and waiting, doubling back when somebody saw us.

Aniza hobbled across from one building to the next. Her feet were heavy like lead and just as loud, but she reached me without alerting anybody. I let out a long-held breath of relief and peered at the terminal. The line was still too long for us to wait in the open.

"What do we do now?" Aniza asked.

"Now, we wait."

She leaned back against the brick of the building. "Oh thank goodness. I needed time to catch my breath."

"It must be hard to be a human surrounded by gods."

She swiveled her head and faced me. "You know how hard it is as much as I do, being a human and all."

I frowned. "I'm not quite a human or a god. I'm something else, and I'm not sure what."

"I'm sure you'll figure it out." She placed her hand on mine.

"I hope so." I patted her hand. "Just sit back and catch your breath. I have a feeling we'll be here for a while."

My instincts were right. I spent the next several hours listening to Aniza's labored breathing until the line was short enough that we would wait for less than five minutes, by my calculations. I nudged Aniza to wake her up.

"This is our best shot."

She looked out with me. "There are still so many."

"We could be waiting for days for the lines to get any shorter. It's your choice, and I can go out myself, but I think we should go together so that I can protect you."

She hesitated, then said, "If you think it's best, then I'll follow your lead."

Even though there were only a couple gods in each queue, all it would take was a look from the wrong people to give us away. I just had to hope that providence was on our side. I wrapped my cloak around Aniza. "Pull it tight."

She flipped up the hood and tied it under her chin, disappearing beneath it. "Thank you."

"Don't thank me. My meddling nearly got you killed. Protecting you is the least I could do."

"You have nothing to apologize for. I'm actually quite excited. I never thought I would see my dear sweet love again."

We moved forward in line as a horse creature vanished into one of the portals. "He might be different from the last time you saw him. You know that, right?"

"I know. Time has changed us both, but simply seeing him again is worth any awkwardness."

The next creature, a hippopotamus with long antlers, disappeared into the portal, and then it was our turn. A tall grasshopper wearing a bellman's cap gave us a bored look. "Where to?"

I handed him the letter Frigg gave me approving our use of the portal. He glanced at it and gave it back, grunting.

"This is for one person. You have two here."

"Oh, really?" I replied. "Is that going to be a problem? What Frigg asked me to acquire requires two people to carry, and so I enlisted my friend."

My heart raced while the grasshopper read the note again. He rubbed his chin and mused, "It does say to afford you every convenience, but this does not approve two—"

"Please," Aniza said. "I know it's irregular, but if you knew what we had to carry, you would let us through post haste."

"And what is that?" he asked. "Now I am curious."

I held my hands out in apology. "I'm sorry, but as the note says, we are on a secret mission of some urgency, and thus, we cannot answer that question. However, I'm sure if I rang Frigg, she would be able to clear this up for us. I'd warn you that she is not a patient woman, and she might kill you for the insolence of denying her. Do you want to take that chance?"

"I know I wouldn't," Aniza added. "And she might kill us, too. The woman is erratic when she gets angry. Who knows, she might bring this whole terminal crumbling to the ground. Is that really a chance you want to take when you could just let us through?"

"Hrm. I guess not." The grasshopper punched the coordinates into a console next to him. "But don't tell anyone, okay?"

"What would we have to gain from that?" I asked. "Our lips are sealed."

"And Frigg thanks you too," Aniza said.

The grasshopper smiled at that and handed me back the paper. "Have a good day."

I pulled Aniza forward, whispering in her ear. "You are a natural liar."

"To survive in this realm, you learn a few things about talking out the side of your mouth."

CHAPTER 47

NIMUE

I needed to talk to Cassandra. I feared my lies would not be enough to dissuade the King in Yellow from taking drastic action, and I needed her to accept a mission that she wasn't going to like. It was too much to ask, but I had no other choice.

I found my maid of honor with Lydia and Delilah, welcoming the wedding guests. Dukes and lords had been shuffling into the castle for the last hour, along with duchesses and ladies. They wore pressed tuxedos and flowing gowns even more extravagant than those I'd seen at the ball when I was captured.

All eyes turned to me as I approached. I was sure they were curious to know how I went from assassin to prisoner to queen. That wasn't going to happen, though, if my plan did not succeed, and it would not succeed without Cassandra's help.

"Cassandra dear," I asked. "May I have a word with you?"

She followed me around to the side of the castle, to the

same rose trellis where I had spoken with Rapunzel. I leaned in close. "King Hastur knows something is wrong."

She went pale. "How do you know?"

"Bethel and Elvira still are not back, and with every passing minute his suspicion grows."

"This is not good," she replied, biting her fingers. "If he takes measures against us, all hope is lost."

"I know." I took a deep breath. "Which is why I need something from you. It is more than I have any right to ask, and you have every right to say no."

The words hung in the back of my throat, so vile were they to even think, let alone say them aloud.

"What is it?" Cassandra asked. "You are scaring me."

"You should be scared," I said. "For what I need you to do is the most despicable thing I could ever ask of another, especially you."

A glint of understanding flickered in her eyes, and she dropped her head. "Whatever you ask of me, I will do."

I swallowed loudly, choking down the guilt that blocked my words. "I need you to offer yourself to the dark lord. Tell him you come as a gift from his queen, to release his tension before the ceremony."

"I know I said anything, but..." She blinked, and then her head rose. "You know what you ask of me, and after what I told you earlier?"

"I do, and it rocks me to my core to do so." I blew out a deep sigh of regret. "I would do it myself, but I must remain strong for what is to come and keep all of my strength. Besides, he would see my submission as an act of weakness, but my gift of you as an act of charity."

"That is horrendous." Delilah appeared behind the trellis and her face said she had been listening the whole time. "The point of all this is so that none of us have to be tortured ever again."

"I know," I replied. "But I don't have another way."

"Let's just go kill him now," Delilah replied.

"We can't, not until Bethel and Elvira come back. They are tracking something down for me that will ensure the king's weakness and give us a better chance of success. Until they return, we are powerless."

"You ask us to trust you," Delilah said. "But then you ask for us to do the one thing…this is not right."

"Nothing is right." I clasped my hands. "I hate all of this as much as you."

"No," Cassandra said. "I hate this more than you, I assure you, but I will do as you ask because I trust you."

Delilah reached for Cassandra's hand. "You don't have to—"

"I will do it for all of you." Cassandra turned to me. "I know that you do not trust me, and you have every right to keep your distance, but I hope that when I do this you will see that I am as trustworthy as all the other princesses."

"You sacrifice yourself for us," Delilah replied. "I will not forget it, and I will be sure they do not either."

I wrapped Cassandra's hands in mine. "You must keep him occupied until it is too close to the ceremony for him to stop it."

"I don't know if I can do that," she said, staring at the ground. "I am not as strong as the others."

"I will go with you. We will face this together," Delilah said.

I shook my head. "No, the last time nearly broke you. I cannot bear that two of my sisters would suffer because of this."

"Then make sure it is worth it," Delilah said, putting

her hand on Cassandra's shoulder. "Together, we are stronger than apart. That is the point of all this, is it not? All for one, one for all, and all that. We cannot hope to live that tomorrow if we do not practice today."

"It is a noble thing you both do. More noble than any I can imagine."

Delilah sniffed. "Remember it when this is over, my queen. Now, we will do as you say. Forgive us if we miss the ceremony."

"You will be forgiven today and every day hence."

She nodded and turned to Cassandra. "Come, let us face our destiny together."

"I am ready, sister."

CHAPTER 48

ARIEL

Whimpers filled the darkness in the hall outside the throne room. Canterbury sat next to me, holding my hand. I was fine, surprisingly, but the cries of the prisoners—children among them— awaiting punishment simply for existing pounded against my ears and weakened my resolve.

Finally, the door creaked open, filling the room with unnatural blue light that elongated the shadows.

"Step forward," said a booming voice, and I knew it was for me.

I marched forward, determined to gather the will for one final push. Canterbury walked beside me as we entered the throne room. At the far end the blue light shone low, which twisted every statue in the room into nightmare creatures. The footsteps of the other prisoners slowed.

"I don't like this," he said.

"Now you are concerned for my well being?" I whispered. "I think it's a little late for that."

From the end of the room, a figure blocked the light, its shadow falling across all of us. "Dream Walker." The words cracked through the air. "I have waited so long for your arrival."

"Shadow King," Canterbury said. "As promised, I have delivered a Dreamer to you."

The pointed helmet of the shadow turned slightly to address my rabbit companion. "You have done well. I am most pleased."

"Thank you Kel—Shadow King." Canterbury knelt to the ground. "Everything I do, I do for your glory, and the glory of the Nightmare Realm."

The Shadow King stepped down from the throne, letting the blue light catch me in the eyes again. I raised my hand to block it and squinted to keep the king of shadows in view.

"And you, Dream Walker. What do they call you?"

"Ariel, sir."

"Ariel, yes. Well, you are a great boon. Has the rabbit told you about what your presence means to Sprig, and this realm?"

I shook my head, not wanting to get my new friend in trouble. "No, but he spoke of your glory at every turn, and that you were the most powerful being in all of The Nightmare Realm."

"He is correct." He slammed something into the ground, and the floor quaked beneath us. I stumbled onto my knees. "Ah, finally you show me the respect I deserve."

The Shadow King was close enough to touch. His long, black robe concealed his form, and all that was visible inside his pointed helmet was his glowing green eyes. A wooden snake coiled around the long staff in his hand and at the top, a green orb glowed the same color as his eyes. Floating motionless in its center was an eye. It had to be Rapunzel's.

The Shadow King held out the tip of his staff and lifted my chin with it. "With you, I will finally fulfill my destiny and open a portal to the Dream Realm."

"Epiales couldn't keep a portal open. What makes you think you will be more successful? We now have Hypnos to protect us."

"Epiales was weak, and Hypnos is a fool. I will bring the whole of the Nightmare Realm to bear on Urgu and it will fall."

"I don't think so!" The familiar voice echoed through the hall. I looked past the Shadow King to see a familiar figure standing in the light.

"Corben!"

"Hi, Ariel!" he replied. "Sorry I couldn't save you, but it's good to see you."

"Oh, don't worry about it. I'm exactly where I want to be."

"What insolence is this?" the Shadow King shouted. "Stop him!"

Monsters appeared out of the shadows, and every twisted form the statues made came to life began to attack the prisoners.

"I'm not alone!" Corben raised his hand, and several dozen people poured into the room. "Attack!"

The prisoners. He had done it. He saved them all, by himself, without me. How I wished I could hear him recount his story, but that was for another time. I had my opening, and I lunged for the Shadow King, tackling him to the ground with all that remained of my strength.

He smashed my ribs with the butt of his staff and rolled away. He sprang to his feet and looked down on me, his eyes glowing intensely, readying to strike me again.

"You dare! Ava—"

"No!" Canterbury kicked at Shadow King. "I can't believe I'm doing this!"

The staff rolled across the ground, and I skittered after it, but my legs fought me like they were bound in thick oatmeal. The light fell from the staff, and the shadow monsters that had appeared from the statues fell to the ground, motionless.

"Get back here!" the Shadow King shouted, but nothing happened. The light had left his eyes, leaving nothing but dull brown in its place.

I summoned one final bit of energy and kicked the Shadow King in the face. He fell back, whelping like a scared puppy, like the Kelvin that Canterbury was convinced still lived inside the evil ruler.

I hobbled forward, my arms and legs heavy like stone, and took the staff. The moment I touched it, a great surge of energy flowed through me, like I had reconnected with a source of power that had been long hidden from me. I lifted it into the air, and with one harsh movement I smashed it to the floor, cracking it into a hundred pieces. The Shadow King wretched backward and let out a billowing, unhuman scream that echoed across the walls of the place before letting out an explosion of magic that shook the castle's foundation.

Huge chunks of the ceiling crashed onto the ground around me. I steeled my resolve through the destruction as I looked through the rubble to find the eye. This would all be useless without it. The castle teetered under its own weight, and I rolled out of the way to avoid a shard of rock hurtling towards me.

My breath came shallow in the panic that swelled in my body, but in that fear came focus. I looked up, in a last desperate attempt to salvage the eye, and spied it a few yards away. I leapt to my feet and lunged forward, grabbing it just as a parapet broke loose from the exposed roof and nearly crushed it, with me underneath.

I jumped out of the way and jammed the eye safely in my pocket, feeling the energy pulsate through my hands and down to my feet in time with the beating of my frantic heart.

Corben scrambled over and pulled me to my feet. "I guess you didn't need my help after all."

"Are you kidding?" I replied. "That was a perfect distraction. You're a hero!"

As I rushed out of the tumbling building, I turned back to see the rabbit kneeling over Kelvin's body. "Come on!"

"I can't leave him!"

I bit my lip, staring at him, then looked over my shoulder at Corben.

"You can't be serious," he said.

"I can't let him die. There is still good in him. I know it."

I sprinted back, and Corben followed me. We loaded the Shadow King onto our arms and rushed out of the hall just as the ceiling caved in. With one final lunge, we made it out the front door. The top of the castle collapsed a split second later.

I looked around, expecting to see hundreds of soldiers descending upon us, but there were none. With the destruction of the staff, the shadow guards must have vanished. Corben grinned at me and the other prisoners, now freed, while Canterbury gently supported his friend's head in his hands. He was no longer the haggard bunny that had chased me, but he wasn't quite one of the fuzzy things that I remembered from the Dream Realm. He was something in the middle.

"Thank you," Canterbury said. "You could have let him die."

I shook my head. "No, I couldn't. That's not how I work."

"It's infuriating," Corben said. "Still, it's effective."

I reached into my pocket and withdrew the eye. "Now it's time to keep my promise to you, to all of you, and bring you somewhere you can be safe."

CHAPTER 49

ROSE

"What have you done?" I hissed at Maricel from across Rama's kitchen. I inched toward her.

"Exactly what we intended. Odin is a powerful ally, but he is still a wildcard. It's so much easier to have him under our control."

I circled her. "And who are you? What are the Spore?"

"We are ancient," Maricel said, her voice now lower and more animalistic. "In the moments after the Big Bang, we were formed in the ooze of the universe. We created all of this, before the gods were even a twinkle of an idea. We favored none, and allowed all to thrive, but the gods saw that as chaos, to which they needed to impose order. They rose up and banished us to the regions outside of time and space, where we waited to return, and now, nothing can stop that from happening."

"That's where you're wrong. Those crystals can kill you."

Maricel chuckled, looking over at the blue crystal bag. "You think this magic will destroy us?"

"I think you're afraid of it, and that is enough for me." I lunged for her. "Give it to me!"

She spun away from my attack and snapped her fingers, raising a dozen knives from the cutting board on the counter. "You humans are so frail."

I dove out of the way to avoid the knives, but not before one of them sliced the back of my leg. I cried out in pain then shrieked. "*Impetum!*"

The knives dislodged from the wall as I directed them toward Maricel. She created a shield out of thin air, and they bounced off.

I didn't need to defeat her. I just needed the crystals. It was then that I remembered how Kadlu told me to activate them. Perhaps if I could banish the spores from Maricel's body, then she would come to my side.

"*Sahaq.*" I held my hand out and the plastic container burst open. The crystal jittered in the air and crumbled into fine dust. "*Rih.*"

The dust exploded into Maricel's face. For a moment she stood straight up like a puppet, and then she crumbled to the ground. Her mouth opened and a cloud of black mold spewed into the air. Then it rose to my height and shot forward.

"*Scotum!*" A blue forcefield surrounded me. The spores bounced off. I held my hands up, ready to cast another spell, but the spore cloud shot directly upward and disappeared into the air ducts.

I ran to Maricel and lifted her head. "Are you okay?"

Her eyes fluttered open. "Oh my gods. It was horrible. Horrible. I can't—you would not believe what they are planning."

"We can talk about it later. Right now we have to get you to safety."

She grabbed my hand and pulled my face close to hers. "You don't understand. They won't stop until they rip a hole in the universe and allow their brethren to pour back into our world. They will stop at nothing to destroy everything the gods have created."

"You can tell me all about it once we get you out of here."

Maricel's eyes went wide when she saw the door open and Rama stepped into the room, carrying a large staff with an orange orb at its head.

"Well, this is very disappointing. Luckily, we have a new ally."

From over his shoulder, Odin materialized. I saw the spores darting back and forth inside his eyes, and I knew I was going to die.

CHAPTER 50
BETHEL

There were too many of them. Every time we finished one monster off, two more took their place. Eventually, we had no choice but to run, and run, and run. Elvira barked out orders as we turned corners at full speed, crashing into walls and each other.

"In here!" she shouted finally.

I slid into the room and slammed the door. Elvira knocked over every piece of furniture we could find to barricade ourselves into the room, but it wouldn't hold long. The monsters were too powerful and the door too weak.

"You're sure it's in here?" I asked, huffing and puffing.

"Absolutely not." She held up the map. "But according to this map, it's in here somewhere."

"Let me see it."

The map was an overview of the whole prison, which meant that it didn't precisely locate the golden locket, just that it was somewhere in the room.

"I can destroy the map and use Issha's blood to locate the locket, but if this isn't the right room, then we will have incinerated it for nothing."

"I don't think you have any other choice," Elvira said, eyeing the door. Monsters pounded against it.

She was right. I placed the map on the floor and crumpled it into a ball, then put my hands on either side of it and spoke the magical words. The paper went up in a ball of flames. As the pieces flaked away, they created a trail leading to the far wall, where the last of the flames landed on one of the bricks.

It loosened when I pressed against it, and so I dug my fingers deep into the mortar and yanked. The brick yielded and fell to the floor. I reached my hand inside and pulled out a yellowed cloth. My gut tightened as I unfurled the cloth. Inside lay the golden locket, tarnished with time, a glowing ruby at its center.

"I have it!" I shouted.

"Good," Elvira replied, straining to hold the door closed. "Now, how do we get out of here?"

I saw our dilemma. There was no exit except for the way we came, which was flooded with a dozen monstrous demons gnashing at us, waiting for their dinner.

"You ask a good question," I replied.

"I have an idea, but it is daft. I honestly can't believe I would even bring it up."

"There are no stupid ideas, except for ideas that are stupid."

"Do you remember Antari?"

I thought back, and then nodded. "Of course. We razed the city for a week, and they would not budge. So Hastur had us—" I realized what she meant. "No, I couldn't do that."

"I have thought it our only possible way out but didn't dare speak it until now."

Antari would not fall to our troops, no matter how

many we threw at it, and our magic was useless against it. The wall surrounding their city was impenetrable, even with an army chipping away at it for weeks. That was when Hastur came up with a new spell, one that would decimate the walls that had stood since time immemorial. It took every bit of our concentration.

"You have no idea if it will work on these demons. It was meant for stone and brick."

"I can use it to cut you a path back to the prison, and the demons will have no choice but to respect it. Even if it doesn't kill them, it will not be pleasant."

My mind raced, playing out the plan. Then it hit a snag. "And how would you get out?"

"That's the thing...I wouldn't."

"No, you cannot sacrifice yourself for me."

Elvira scoffed. "Why not? We had no affections for each other before this day, and what matters is the death of the King in Yellow. If we do not return with that locket, then we would doom all our sisters to a fate worse than death."

"And you would die."

"Maybe, but it is a far cry better than living under Hastur's terror." The door splintered beneath the monsters' claws. "Do you remember the spell to protect yourself from the attack?"

"I do." Pain twisted my stomach, and tears fell from my face. I reached up and touched one of them. "I have not cried since my parents died."

"And do not shed them for me. I have done nothing worthy of tears my whole life, and I do not want or need them now."

"Don't do this."

"I won't have you telling me what to do. I have been

under the thumb of another for far too long. I will think for myself at the end. Now, ready yourself."

She let out a foul scream, turning yellow. I pressed my hand to my chest and shouted the incantation that would protect me from the light. My body glowed a deep red until an enormous pillar of light shot from Elvira's body through the door. The monsters scattered, howling, as the light crashed through them.

I stepped through the hole in the wall. The muscles and sinew that made up the walls undulated in pain as her screech pierced the air, and the monsters sprinted along, seeking shelter. I pounded my legs as fast as I could while the prison itself worked to stop me in my tracks. But I would not let it. I kicked harder until I made my way to the stairs. A few of the monsters nipped at my heels as I climbed and leapt through the door.

Baba laid on the floor, shrieking in pain. The prison was tied to her, and Elvira's spell cut at her insides. I smiled. It wasn't my intention to destroy the old crone this day, but it was a nice bonus.

Now, I needed to return to the castle before the ceremony and find a way to explain away Elvira's disappearance.

CHAPTER 51

ROSE

"Hurry up!" I shouted. A magical bolt exploded next to us. We snaked our way through the kitchen and I flung a force-field behind me. "That won't hold them for long!"

"There's a way out down the stairs," Maricel called back over her shoulder as she led me through the servant dining room and down a flight of narrow stairs. The last time I took these stairs it was with Red, when we discussed how to save Rama. Now I was running from him. The ceiling exploded just as we reached the basement, dust and debris raining down.

Rama leapt down after us. "You can't run, Rose," he said, holding a large staff with a glowing orb at the top. "You have outlived your usefulness."

"And what was that? Bringing Odin around so you could poison him?"

"Something like that," Rama replied. "You played your part beautifully. Now, we have a powerful ally."

"You're not a god anymore," Maricel said, wheeling on him. "And I am."

He slammed the staff into the ground and his eyes

glowed orange with it. "Luckily, I gathered plenty of magical items for just this type of eventuality. Now, if you do—"

"*Fulgar!*" I was sick of Rama pontificating. I had always hated him, and now I had a reason to fry him.

A strike of lightning shot through him, and he screamed wildly. Now that he was nothing but a simple human, he was no match for me.

"Enough!" Maricel shouted, grabbing my arm. "You can't kill him!"

"That's exactly what I plan to do," I said. "Something I've wanted to do for a long, long time."

"We can still save him." Maricel knelt next to Rama. "When I tell you to, incinerate whatever comes out of him."

"We don't have time for—"

"He's not evil!" she shouted. "I'm not leaving here without him. My sister loves him, and I love her. So, you can go yourself or you can help me, but I will not abandon him."

I felt the love in her voice, and the fear. It was the same blend of emotion I had for Chelle, my dear sweet Chelle. "Okay."

She placed her hands on either side of his body and gurgled an incantation from the back of her throat. Her eyes turned red, and Rama choked and sputtered when the light filled him. His chest jerked, and then a cloud of black spores vomited from his mouth, looking for something—respite, escape, or a new host. It didn't matter because I wouldn't let them find one.

"*Uro!*" The spell was simple to speak, but it created a complex collection of fire from my palms hotter than any I had felt in my life. The walls began to curl. Maricel covered

Rama's body as the fire engulfed the spores and they screeched for relief, but there would be none.

When it was over, the room was on fire, and Maricel pulled Rama onto her back. He was unconscious, but still drew breath, shallow as they were.

"Come on," she said, brushing past me.

I followed her to the safe room and when we were inside, she touched the console, revealing a computer panel. The panel turned from red to green when she placed her hand on it and the whole of the room quaked.

She closed her eyes as the room cut through the ground to the safety above. "I hoped I never had to use this elevator. It meant that everything had gone to pot."

"Did you build it before—" I didn't have the words to properly express her imprisonment by the spores. "Or after?"

"I knew everything it did to me. I was conscious the whole time, but I couldn't do anything to stop it, no matter how much I tried. I know everything they plan, and it is horrible. We must get to Kadlu."

"That's as safe a place as any," I replied.

The room jittered to a stop, and Maricel pushed open the door. She took one step outside and stopped, her face frozen in fear. Odin towered over us, his eyes glowing blue, fire and lightning churning in his hands.

"This is over now," he hissed. "You have caused quite a bit of a commotion, but nothing that can't be fixed. Come quietly, all of you, and I will allow you to live."

"What you did to me wasn't living," Maricel growled. "I would rather die than let you take control of me again."

"That can be arranged."

Odin raised his hands in the air, but he did not fire. Instead, his sneer turned into a look of pure pain. He looked over his shoulder, let out a gasp, and then fell to the ground writing, a golden dagger stuck into his back. He let out one final gasp and dropped dead.

"Get away from my fiancée," Chelle growled.

"Chelle!" I shouted, leaping over Odin's lifeless body to wrap my arms around her. "You're alive!"

"Yes, I'm alive, or at least I think I am. Are you okay?"

I kissed her. "Are you serious? You're alive. I could jump to the moon in joy."

"I'd like to see that."

Maricel cleared her throat. "Not to spoil the reunion, but we need to get going before the whole of the Celestial Realm is out to get us."

"Who's this?" Chelle asked.

"A friend." I looked Maricel over. "At least I think she is."

"Think later," Maricel said. "I can get us out of this realm, but we need to go now."

CHAPTER 52

ARIEL

"Rest here," Corben said. We'd put a day's walk between us and the castle.

The group of us was large, at least fifty or so people between the prisoners, the Shadow King Kelvin, Canterbury, Corben, and me. The prisoners holding Kelvin tossed the former king to the ground, and Canterbury rushed to his side.

"Hey!" the rabbit shouted. "Leave him alone!"

"Why?" Corben asked. "He tortured, imprisoned, and killed my friends. Why should we show him any mercy?"

"Because we are not like him," I answered, turning to the group. "We are better than him, and we cannot fight hate with hate. Only love can fight hate."

A burly prisoner grunted. "I'm not loving this son of a bitch."

"Watch yer mouth!" Canterbury growled. "Or I'll get my Seeker out on you."

"Hey!" Corben shouted. "Both of you stop it! You don't have to respect the Shadow King, but you surely will respect Ariel. She's the only reason you're free right now."

"We both know that's not true," I said. "You saved them. I just smashed a staff."

"A staff destroyed all the shadows and gave us freedom. Do not downplay it."

"You are the real hero." I walked over to him. "How did you save them? That castle seemed impenetrable."

He rubbed his chin. "I knew where they would take you, and that I would need an army to save you. You're right, the castle is heavily guarded, but the mountain it sat on was craggily, and easily climbable."

"It must have been a hundred feet of vertical climbing," Canterbury said in astonishment.

"I counted more like two hundred," Corben said, a glint of a smile on his face. "But I have scaled more difficult. I used to live in a crater, after all. Once I got to the top of the mountain, it wasn't hard to get inside. No one was guarding the back gates. The Shadow King's forces were all concentrated on a frontal assault."

"Of course!" Kelvin said. "How stupid."

"Quiet!" I shouted. "What then?"

"There were surprisingly few guards in the castle. Maybe because shadows only exist in the light and it was nearly pitch black in there, but I made it to the dungeon with ease and freed the prisoners. It was honestly a bit too easy. I thought I would be ambushed before—" He stopped for a moment to look over at Kelvin, and then back to me. "But we weren't. The biggest problem was getting back out to safety again. Many of the prisoners are weak and unable to scale down a mountain, so we decided to fight our way out by smashing every light we could find along the way. I made it to the armory and gave them all the weapons and armor that I could find, and...well, you know the rest. We were just about to smash the light in the throne room when I heard your voice."

"I can't believe you came for me," I said, breathless.

"I would do anything for you." Corben smiled, before his mouth turned down and his eyes found Kelvin's. "What are you going to do to him?"

I knelt down by the former king. "It seems to me like the thing you want more than anything is to return to the Dream Realm. Is that right?"

Kelvin glared. "What's it to you?"

"I just so happen to be going there, and that's where I plan to bring all these poor souls. Would you like to come with us?"

"Why would you do something like that for me?" he asked, still glaring.

"I'm not sure if what I'm offering is a kindness." I took a deep breath. "Once we get through the portal, I will bring you before Hypnos, and he will decide what's best to do with you."

"And what if he lets the criminal go?" a slender red-headed woman asked.

"Hypnos is no fool," I replied. "He will likely imprison him, but it is not my judgement to make, or yours. I will not be burdened with this monster's soul, and I will not allow yours to be tarnished with it, either."

"Are you sure about this?" Corben muttered.

"I'm not sure about anything, but Hypnos has ruled for eons. I will not claim to know more than a god. If anyone has the wisdom to decide what to do with this man, it is him."

"And what if you can't bring us back?" he asked, standing next to me now.

I placed my hand in his. "Are you doubting me?"

"No, I suppose not. Not after what I have seen you do."

"Good," I replied. "Then let's take a break, and we'll get back to it in an hour."

"As you command, my lady," Corben said with a smirk. "Anything for you."

CHAPTER 53
NIMUE

I heard Cassandra and Delilah screaming down the hall from my suite as Lydia helped me into my wedding gown. The pain was the point, after all. Hastur wanted to fill the halls with the torture of my princesses to show I had no power over him, and to give me a preview of what was to come later that evening.

"We should stop him," Lydia said, lacing up my corset. The tailor had finished the final alterations, and while I didn't agree with Hastur's insistence on perfection at all costs, the hand-stitched dress was stunning. I admired the detail of flowers and vines weaving up the tress into the bodice.

"If we stop them now, we will have lost our chance."

Yesterday, I had five bridesmaids to do my bidding. Now I was left with only Lydia, who held a tenuous allegiance with me. She made known her displeasure, mercilessly tightening the corset.

"We trusted you, and you have done nothing but send my sisters into harm's way again and again," she said through gritted teeth.

"They are my sisters, too."

"Maybe," Lydia said. "But you only just got here. I have known them for longer than an age."

"You didn't even talk to them until I arrived." My forced exhalations from her yanking the cords punctuated my words. "You only care for them now because of me and what I have done. Perhaps you could give me the benefit of the doubt."

"I have never given any that privilege, and I will not start with you." She stopped her hands after one final tug. "There you are, as beautiful as any I have ever seen, though you don't deserve it."

"None of us deserve this. That is the point." I stepped down from the pedestal to address Lydia. The dress cascaded down my legs like a field of flowers. "What Delilah and Cassandra are enduring now ensures that none will ever have to endure it again."

"If we succeed."

"And if we do not, their punishment will feel like child's play to what the dark king has in store for us." I held out my hands. "I feel the guilt, too, but we have our part to play. The final strike must come from us, for none other will have the strength to do so. That is our burden."

A crack came from the window, and a flash along with it. When it dissipated, Bethel knelt on the ground, gasping for air.

"Bethel!" I ran over to her. "You have returned."

She spread out her hands to show us the golden locket. It shimmered in the light, even though it was tarnished, and the ruby shined brilliantly. "And I am victorious."

"It is good to see you, sister," Lydia said.

"And you as well," Bethel replied. "Where are the others?"

I avoided the question, instead reaching for the locket. Bethel let it fall from her hand into mine. It throbbed in my fingers, pulsating like the heart in my chest. The clasps that held it shut sizzled when I touched them. "Ow."

"I tried that already. It must be bound with magic. Issha said it must be joined with its master, so I believe it will only yield to the King in Yellow's touch."

"How will we do that? It's not like he is the cuddly type."

"In the ceremony, he will place a ring on your finger to signify his claim to you," Lydia said. "In return, you will wrap a string around his finger the same as your dress, to signify he can pull your heart open for himself. When he reaches out his hand, wrap this around his finger, and hope that it goes the way we want."

"It is as good a plan as any." I held the locket tightly in my hand. "Now, we just have to keep him from finding out until then."

Lydia spoke up. "Where is Elvira?"

Bethel bit her lip. "She sacrificed herself to save me...to save us all. She is a hero."

"We will sing songs about her in the new order," I replied, solemnly.

"And where are Delilah and Cassandra?" A scream echoed through the room and Bethel's face fell when she saw me flinching at the sound. "Do not tell me—"

"We had to distract him somehow. This was the only way I could think."

Bethel clenched her fists. "We were supposed to protect them—protect all of us."

"I'm sorry," I said. "I failed."

"No," she said, swallowing a tear. "It is my failure, and I will fix it."

She stormed out of the room, and when I followed her Lydia blocked me from the door. "You have more important things to worry about, Nimue. As you said, we have our part to play in this yet."

I blew out my breath, defeated. "Of course, and it's not to run off half-cocked."

She shook her head. "That is no way to kill a king."

CHAPTER 54

ARIEL

Both Canterbury and Corben were excellent trackers, and together they led us back to the exact spot where I made it through the divide. As we neared it, the power vibrating from the eye intensified.

"Are you really going to take us all through the portal with you?" Kelvin asked. No longer under the thrall of the Shadow King, his face had softened in the days of our travels, and while none trusted him, they wouldn't hurt him when he was under my, and Canterbury's, protection. "Even me, who caused so much pain?"

"Your greatest wish was to get to the Dream Realm, was it not? You told me it was what drove everything you did."

He nodded. "It is everything I have ever wanted since I found out I could never leave this place."

"Then, I think I can give you your wish. I warn you, though: Hypnos is a harsh, cold god who will not take it easy on you."

"That is fine," he said. "I will submit to his judgment if it allows me to escape this place."

"The Dream Realm isn't magical—or, it is, but it won't

solve all your problems." I called out to the collection of fifty or so refugees traveling with us. "That goes for all of you. It is better than the Nightmare Realm in many ways, but it has its problems, too, and you will still travel by yourself, no matter where you go. It will not make you a different person, lest you make it so."

"That was a nice speech," Corben said with a smile. "But you must be out of your mind if you think leaving the Nightmare Realm won't fix my problems, because literally every one of my problems is caused by this horrible place."

I raised my eyebrows. "You might be surprised. Now, if you'll excuse me. I think it's time I go home."

I didn't know what I was doing, and yet, somehow, the eye guided me to the center of the field. There were neon plants, just like I remembered, but those plants were everywhere in the Nightmare Realm.

The eye rose into the air without my assistance, even though I still held it in my hand. My fingers shook with its energy. Though there was nothing next to me, I felt a powerful force coming from a few feet ahead. I knew it was the other eye, trying to join its estranged mate. A wave of force pushed me back. As I stumbled, the portal rose high into the air in the exact same way it had when I first entered the Nightmare Realm.

"I don't think I can keep it open if I go through," I said to Corben. "You have to get everyone through, and I'll come after you all are safely on the other side."

"If you think that's best," he said, and began gathering the lost souls. They stared at the portal with wide eyes.

"It's okay," I told them. "I will hold it open for you. Freedom is on the other side. Once we return to the Dream Realm, I will introduce you to Hypnos, and we will bring you to the Obsidian Spindle, where you can speak with the Fates about your future."

"That sounds nice," one of them said. She was a little girl, though I knew her to be over seventy years old. Souls never aging was a brutal part of both our realms. "I'll see you on the other side, I guess."

She went through, and with her bravery, others followed, one by one or holding hands, until the only ones left were Corben, Kelvin, Canterbury, and me.

"Do you think I can really be a good person?" Kelvin asked.

"If you want to be, Kelvin," Canterbury replied. "I think you can be anything."

Kelvin squeezed his friend's hand. "We can be anything."

"Not me." Canterbury shook his head. "I'm not going with you. Your reign of terror may be over, but there's a lot of animals you hurt, and I aim to help them if I'm able."

Kelvin's mouth opened and closed before he managed to say, "I can't start over without you. It's too hard."

"You ruled a whole realm, Kelvin," Canterbury replied. "You can do anything. Now go."

"Come on," Corben said. "I'll go through with you."

Kelvin gave him a suspicious look. "You're not going to kill me, are you?"

"Time will tell, but not today." Corben held out his hand.

The two of them disappeared into the light. Even though I would see him in a moment, my heart ached seeing Corben leave. I had grown close to him in the days following the destruction of the Shadow King's castle.

"I hope it works out between the two of you," Canterbury said, watching me.

"I hope it works out for you here. Are you sure you won't come? I can't come back for you."

"It's a stupid decision, but it's mine to make. Besides, I don't think people would accept me over there. Not after what Epiales did."

"You might be surprised. People have an enormous capacity to forgive."

"Some people," the rabbit said. "Thank you for bringing Kelvin with you. There's nothing but danger for him here. Now that he's powerless, every monster in the Nightmare Realm will be after him."

"Happy to do it," I replied. "After all, everyone deserves a second chance, and a third one, and a tenth after that. I'm hopelessly optimistic like that."

"Not hopelessly," Canterbury said. "Your outlook is what saved my friend, and it's what makes me believe I can make a difference here."

"I hope you do."

My hand shook violently as the eye pulled me closer to the portal. "I suppose this is goodbye."

"Have a good life, Ariel. You deserve it."

I waved a final goodbye to Canterbury and then fell into the portal, ready to return to the Dream Realm and start my new life, with whatever challenges and joys that brought.

CHAPTER 55
BETHEL

I didn't know what I would do when I reached Hastur's suite, just that I would not allow him to hurt my sisters for one more moment longer. I left this place ready to betray my sisters but now, after witnessing Elvira selflessly give her life for me, I had a deeper appreciation for them. We would either live or die together, and no matter what I had thrown my lot in with them.

I stormed inside without waiting for permission. There, whimpers and screams were even more pronounced and painful to hear. The door slammed closed, and two orange eyes appeared in the abyss.

"You have returned."

I should have thought more about what would happen when I finally had him within my grasp, but I simply froze. "Yes, your majesty."

The eyes moved closer. Two figures stood on either side, their backs heaving.

"It is good to see you. Tell me, how was flower picking?"

Elvira died for our cause. She deserved better than the lie that formed on my lips. "You were right, my liege. There was a plot against you. However, it did not come from the queen to be. It came from Elvira. She worked against you for years and knew that I would be your ally. She tried to convince me to turn on her, but I did not."

"Did you finish her?"

I looked down at my feet. "I wish I had brought you back her head, but I'm afraid there is nothing but dust left of it."

"Hrm," Hastur's eyes bobbed around the room. "That makes sense as to why you were in Baba's woods."

"Yes, your majesty. She insisted on teleporting us, even though I knew exactly where we were going. She brought a terrible monster to bear down on me. I only barely escaped with my life, and then, weakened, she took me to Baba." *Did any of this even make sense?* "It took all my cunning, but I was able to escape. Elvira followed me. That is when we had our final battle and, as you know, none are a match for me in battle."

Hastur stayed silent for a long while. If he didn't believe me, then I would be as good as dead, and he would know we were all lying to him. I was a good liar when necessary, however; I layered just enough truth to make it believable.

"I am not one for trusting," the King in Yellow said. "But you have been so loyal to me, for so long, even when all others who have long abandoned me, that I find it hard not to believe your words. Are you sure that no others conspire against me?"

I nodded. "I was the first one she tried to turn. She said that with me on her side the others would fall in line."

The eyes narrowed. "Do you have any idea why she chose to make her stand now?"

"Maybe she was insulted that you would take another

for a wife, or maybe she saw the distraction as an opportunity."

"I admit, my mind has been on other things."

I caught a glimpse of the two silhouettes. "I did see Nimue on my way here. She asked if you are done with her maidens, as they are needed for the wedding."

Hastur laughed. "She is cold blooded to have them stand with her after all I have done to them."

"Perhaps she is a good match for you after all."

"Perhaps." His eyes turned in the direction of the whimpering. "Very well. They can go."

"Wonderful."

He reached out to them and muttered a spell, and the two figures glowed yellow. The whimpering stopped after that. "Don't say I was not magnanimous to give you your health back. Now, get out of my sight before I change my mind."

A pattering of feet passed me, and the door opened. I barely caught sight of two naked bodies as they rushed out of the room. With any luck, they would tell Nimue everything and allow us to straighten our stories.

"I have a request to make of you, Bethel." Hastur paused for a moment. "In all my years as a king, I have relied on few, but you have never let me down. I would like you to walk with me down the aisle, and then stand by my side when I say my vows. Will you do this for me?"

I bowed. "Of course, my king. It would be my honor."

CHAPTER 56

RED

The portal spat us out on a vibrant planet covered in lush grass and flowers up to my knees. A small house, not unlike the one that Aniza occupied until recently, stood in the meadow with me. The door to the Spindle closed with a slam, but the light remained from a sun that shone overhead. It was an idyllic setting fit for a vacation or retirement.

"I guess this is the place, huh?" I asked.

Aniza looked around. "Maybe, if Odin gave you the right location."

I expected a bunch of dragons or monsters guarding the key maker, but all that separated me from him was a blue door. I knocked on it and heard shuffling inside.

"Who is it?" a voice crowed.

"Gabrielle...you don't know me, but I brought a woman who knows you."

I held Aniza's necklace to the peephole, and then pulled Aniza in front of it. There was a gasp on the other side of the door, and it swung open. The man standing there wore high-waisted pants with a yellow, green, and orange checkered shirt and rainbow suspenders.

"Aniza?" He adjusted his glasses. "Is that you?"

She shook her head. "Oh, Shaun. You poor fool."

In one swift motion, Aniza pulled out a pistol and fired it twice at the key maker. I spun my brahmastra in a circle and knocked the pistol out of her hand. "What are you doing?"

The figure morphed into a tall woman with purple hair and pink skin. "You are very gullible. I thank you for that."

"Who are you?" I asked. "Who sent you? What did you do to Aniza?"

"Killed her, of course. You saw her—oh wait, you only saw what I wanted you to see. As for who sent me, let's just say I work for a group who doesn't want the Dark Planet opened again, and leave it at that." She pulled out two daggers. "Especially since you'll be dead in a couple of seconds."

She lunged at me, and I spun the brahmastra. The longer I wielded it in battle, the lighter it became. The assassin was quick, but she was no match for a weapon powerful enough to make Rama a god. Every attack I parried, firing my daggers to keep the attacker off balance.

"You're better than I thought."

I held the brahmastra at the ready. "You don't have to die today. Tell me who you work for, and I will simply torture you for a while."

"You'll find out quickly enough, if you survive that long."

She swung at me again, and I spun the brahmastra around with such force that it sliced the woman in half. My unanswered questions would have to wait until I found the key.

Shaun was bleeding profusely when I reached him. I cradled his head, saying, "No, no, no. You can't die."

He chuckled. "I promise you, gods can die as well as the rest. Just we have nowhere to go afterwards." He coughed. "You are looking for the key."

"I am."

"Then you are a fool. I hid it where it could never be used by any god for their own gain."

I held up the brahmastra. "I brought this. You can use it to make another key when you get better."

"Do you really think it was a lack of material that prevented me from making another? I have all I ever needed. That was just a lie I told to keep those seeking me at bay." He looked over at the assassin's body. "I was so blind. I should have known Aniza would never put me in harm's way—"

His breath was labored, and I grabbed the sides of his shirt. "No, old man. Tell me where the key is!"

He laughed again. "When he was made by the two, I gave them the power to control their destiny. If only they could take it."

His eyes rolled back in his head as I shook him. "Wait, that doesn't make any sense! What does it mean?"

But it was no use. Shaun was dead, and with him went my chances of opening the door to the Dark Planet. As he went limp, his hand fell from his chest, revealing half of a locket, a perfect match for the one Aniza gave me.

CHAPTER 57
NIMUE

It was time.

My wedding had arrived. I stood in the unlit hallway outside the great hall with Lydia, Cassandra, Delilah, shrouded in darkness. My heart thumped a thousand beats a minute. In less than an hour, we would either be free, or condemned, and it depended completely on me which one it would be.

I passed the locket to Cassandra. "Keep this until the right moment, okay?"

She nodded. "I will."

I placed my hand on her shoulder. "I'm so sorry that I—"

"Don't," she replied. "If you start blubbering, it will ruin your make-up. Just don't mess this up, okay? Do this right and all will be forgiven."

The music swelled and the doors creaked open, bathing us in bright white light. I squared my shoulders. "Let's do this."

Cassandra stood on my left, Delilah on my right, and Lydia walked behind, making sure the train of my dress didn't catch on anything. The procession stepped over the archway of the great hall and the assembled dignitaries stood to face us. They were hideous, monstrous creations, and I would be responsible for them if I succeeded.

They smiled as I passed, and I tipped my head to them solemnly before turning my attention to the platform in the center of the room. The dark lord Hastur stood in a hooded robe as intricately designed as my dress, the yellow of it masked by dark, monstrous shadows with glowing eyes. Next to him stood Bethel, looking stoic. I wanted to reach out and thank her for doing what I could not, but she was deep in focus. Between them was a dryad made from a gnarled tree standing with a red robe the color of fire, shimmering in the light.

I realized, as we walked to the stage, that the orbs illuminating the room were the same ones that burned me when I proposed to Hastur in his quarters. If anything went wrong, they would douse the assembly in liquid hot magma. He really was one for the dramatic.

"Good eve, queen," Hastur said as I took my place. He walked forward to raise my black veil, a tradition on the Dark Planet to contrast the white of the dress. "You look ravishing, and I certainly intend to feast upon you later."

I curtsied. "I am so pleased you approve, your highness."

The dryad cleared its throat. "We are here to celebrate the union between King Hastur and Princess Nimue, in unholy matrimony. If you would please sit."

The tension in the room was palpable as everyone sat down and began to shift in their seats. The dryad made a blessing and did a reading, but all I could think about was Hastur's hand. I would only have a moment to perform my impossible task, and his bony fingers made a small target.

"Nimue?" The dryad's voice knocked me out of my trance.

"Yes, Father?" I replied, then murmured, "Is that what they call you?"

"You can call me whatever you would like, my queen. Are you ready for the vows?"

"Yes, Father."

"Do you swear fealty to the dark lord for all time, putting him above all others, forsaking everything you believed in before meeting him, to prostrate yourself before him, every day of your life, and into the great beyond, and never willingly see harm come to him?"

I bit the inside of my cheek. "I do."

The dryad turned to Hastur. "And do you, your excellence, accept this wretch as your own, to do with what you will, for the rest of her days?"

"I accept this offering graciously," he said.

"Then take this ring, and with it, bind her to your will, until she no longer pleases you." The dryad made the sign of a pentagram. The ring in his hand glowed green, then changed from a rose gold to a dark black.

My eyes went wide. "What are you doing?"

"Binding the magical contract, my dear?" Hastur said with an evil smile. "You can't expect me to simply trust you will be loyal and faithful, do you? Not with a will as strong as yours."

I felt the princesses holding their breath around me. I couldn't let that ring touch my finger. If I did, everything we worked for would be forfeit. I reached my hand out to Cassandra. Reading my mind, she gave me the locket. I went to latch it onto him but when I did, he moved his free hand and slapped it away with a low growl.

"I'm so disappointed in you." He looked around the room. "In all of you."

All the lights fell to the floor with a motion of his hand, soaking the crowd in hot liquid and darkening the room so I could not see.

All was lost. We were as good as dead.

No, Hastur would never let us die.

Then, Bethel did something I didn't expect, and kicked Hastur backwards into the dryad. "No, it is I who am disappointed in you. Get the locket! We'll hold him off for as long as we can."

"Fools!" Hastur shouted. "I made you, and I can destroy you all the same!"

"You didn't create me!" a voice shouted that I recognized from the other side of the great hall.

"Elvira!" Bethel shouted. "You're alive!"

"I'm afraid not, my dear," the voice said. "But her body is a powerful vessel for me."

"Baba," I whispered.

"Yes." She snapped her fingers and The Faceless Woman appeared next to her. "Now, let us end this and correct my sister's and my great bane."

CHAPTER 58

ARIEL

I knew something was wrong when the portal to the Dream Realm collapsed, but I thought with it reopening, whatever horror existed beyond had been resolved. I was not prepared for what I witnessed when I returned through the portal.

"Welcome back, dear."

Nox, the goddess of the dark, stood with Hypnos bound at her feet. Around her, dust rose into the air.

"What did you do to my friends?" I asked, the words heavy on my tongue. I had seen death come to Urgu before, and understood all too well that the dust hanging in the air was the remnants of my friends.

Still, I did not want it to be true. I was desperate to believe that something, anything else happened to them, but even as the words escaped my lips, I knew it was simply blind, foolish hope that made me say them.

"I killed them, of course." She smiled a toothy grin that knocked the wind out of my body. "They were inconsequential. Where you are going, it's better if you don't have any attachments."

Tears fell from my face. "You killed them? I'll kill you!"

I charged her, but she didn't flinch. She simply raised her hand and flung me against the rock wall with a flick of her finger.

"Oh, you poor child. You are all, each of you, already dead. You live at my whim, and the whim at the behest of my idiotic children. All of this is fantasy. So, while I dealt the final blow to your friends, they already died on Earth. I just disposed of them."

It was all worthless, all of it. None of what I had done made any difference at all. I always looked at the best of the world, but it was all taken from me. Corben, Kelvin, the children I'd promised a better life. I lied to them. They would have been better off in the Nightmare Realm. Here, they didn't even have a chance.

"Now, where is the eye?" Nox asked, sauntering over.

The eye. That was something I had, and maybe the only thing that could rival Nox's power. I felt it in my hand and raised it into the air. However, before I could cast a spell I felt a great pull on my arms, and it was ripped away. Nox caught it without effort.

"Fabulous." She walked to Hypnos and kicked him in the stomach. "My son thought that he could keep me from it by closing off the portal, but I knew you would find a way to bring it back. You have always been trustworthy that way, you little eager beaver."

"I can't believe I ever called you friend."

She laughed. "Well, that was your fault for being so gullible. I am a goddess. I would never sully myself with your friendship. Still, you have some use to me."

Nox snapped her fingers and I rose to my feet despite myself. I struggled against it, but it was useless. I was clay in her hands, to be molded at her whim. She lifted her finger, and a charge of light flowed through me. I glowed a faint yellow.

"What are you going to do to me?" I feigned bravery, but my words cracked as they danced on the air, finding purchase through the grey flecks of my friends.

"Something wonderful." She stepped forward. "You should be happy. You'll meet your friends in oblivion soon. But first, I have a very important job for you."

She snapped her fingers again, and I fell into the black. I didn't know where I would wake up, or if I would, but I had no hope for salvation.

CHAPTER 59

ROSE

Maricel led us through the city to a small house, dilapidated compared to those around it. The door was open, and an old woman laid on the floor, her blood pooling across the warped floorboards.

"Did you kill this woman?" I asked.

Maricel shook her head. "No, of course not. I'm not a monster."

"Then why are we here?" Chelle asked.

"It's weird." Maricel scratched her head. "It's like when the spores vanished from my brain, I remembered this place, like a lock had been placed upon it by somebody." She placed Rama on the floor and knelt down by the woman. "Poor Aniza. What have they done to you?"

"No offense to that dead person," Chelle said. "But this place clearly isn't safe, so can we get a move on?"

"Rude," I said. "Can you have some empathy?"

"I will have all the empathy in the world when we are off the Celestial Realm and the literal army of people chasing us."

Maricel let a single tear fall onto Aniza's body. "No, she's right. It's downstairs."

"What is?"

"The Spindle."

Maricel grabbed Rama and led us down a tight stairwell. The room underneath was little more than concrete and stone, but in the center of it was a miniature version of an Obsidian Spindle, just like the one I found in the palace gardens in Hell.

However, this one was covered in dust. "It isn't charged. This is going to take a lot of my energy. Rose, come here and help me. You too, Chelle."

"I'm not helping you do anything until you tell me what—"

"Do you want to get off this planet or not," I said, cutting Chelle off. I walked over to her. "I admit I shouldn't trust everyone I do, but she's saved us already, so I choose to trust her."

Maricel set Rama down and looked at Chelle. "It's not going to be enough without you. You're like a huge magical battery."

"I'm not helping y—"

"Just do it, Chelle," I butted in again. "We don't have time to argue. We really need to get out of here."

She scowled. "Fine."

Chelle and I touched the Spindle where Maricel told us. "Close your eyes and imagine my sister's planet," Maricel said, with her hands on either side of the Spindle.

I did as she asked, and imagined the world covered in acid rain that Kadlu lived on. "Make it as specific as possible. If you don't picture it perfectly, we could jump into the middle of a black hole or a dying planet."

"No pressure." I imagined every blade of grass and piece

of dirt until it was as real as the floor I stood on. "Okay. I've got it."

My hands pulsated as Maricel muttered a spell to herself. Heat filled me, and then it shot forward through my fingertips into the Spindle, which flashed with light.

"It worked!" I shouted.

Maricel picked up Rama. "Let's hope you did it right. Go first. I'll close it behind us and destroy the Spindle so nobody can find us."

"Are you sure that's a good idea? I mean, we might need it again."

"Whoever is after you knows about this place, as evidenced by the dead woman upstairs, so no, I don't think it's a good idea to keep it open."

"Fair enough," Chelle held out her hand to me. "Are you ready to go?"

I grabbed her hand and squeezed it. "Absolutely."

I held my breath until we were through the portal. A ways off, I saw the skyline of Kadlu's city. Then, in a flash of light and a quake of thunder, Kadlu appeared in front of us, as if she had felt Rama on the air.

"You're back!" Kadlu's eyes were full of hope but lined with fear. "Did it work? Did you—" She must have seen my downturned face then. "What happened?"

"We did save him, but—"

Maricel walked through the portal, holding Rama on her shoulders. "It's done—sister, I didn't expect to see you here."

Kadlu smiled. "I didn't expect to see you ever again. Is it really you? And is that...Rama?"

Maricel slid Rama to the ground. "He is hurt, but alive."

"And the spores?"

"They are gone, from both of us."

Kadlu threw her hand over her mouth. "You too? I didn't even think—I'm sorry for leaving you like that. If I ever thought—I am so ashamed."

"It's okay, sister. There is nothing you could do, and now I am here. We are together again."

Kadlu brushed Rama's cheek. "He no longer has the glow of a god."

"That's because he betrayed me," Chelle said. "Good riddance."

"It wasn't him, Chelle," I replied. "It was the Spore."

Maricel nodded. "It's true. He was a sweet god before. This was all the Spore's doing."

"What is the Spore?" Chelle looked at each of us.

"They are a sentient collective. They are a harbinger of death from those that ruled the universe before the gods, and they have decided now is the time to enact their terrible plan."

"How do you know that?" Kadlu asked.

"I remember everything from when I was connected to them," Maricel said. She had a faraway look on her face. "They moved individually, but also as one. They guide our actions, but they also have our memories. They leech on them to survive, and their consciousness seeps into ours until we are nothing but a vessel to them."

"What are they planning?" I asked.

Maricel stood up. "There was a woman of legend. She found a way to steal the power of the Primordials from the gods. They called her Rapunzel. She managed to tap into the Source of all power, the same source the gods use, and use it for her gain. She was punished for her actions and sent to the Dark Planet, but Nox, the goddess of dar—"

I held up my hand. "We know her."

"Right. Well, Nox found Rapunzel's secret. She planned

to use it to give everyone in the universe powers and end the reign of the gods forever."

"But then Zeus found out," Chelle said.

Maricel nodded. "And the information found its way to Rama, who realized the same power could be used to tear a hole in the universe and let the Primordials back in, to wreak havoc and claim what was once theirs."

"That's horrible," Kadlu said. "I never thought—I was too focused on Rama."

"No, what is horrible is that Nox was captured, and that put her in Rama's hands. Zeus held him off for a while—"

"Until Red killed him," I said.

"Yes, and with that, Nox was turned over to Rama, who filled her with spores, and now everything she knows, they all know." Maricel pointed to Chelle. "You are the key to this, as is your friend Red. If they get the two of you and find a way to the Dark Planet. This is all over."

I stepped forward, my hands balled into fists. "I'm not letting them take Chelle, no matter what."

"Thanks, Rose," Chelle said, kissing my cheek. "If I have to fight the gods, then there's nobody else I'd rather have on my side."

Kadlu stood and turned to me. "Luckily, I've been preparing for this day for a long time."

CHAPTER 60

BETHEL

Baba shot a stream of light toward Hastur's body. It infuriated me that she had draped herself in Elvira's skin, but now was not the time to forcibly rip it from her.

"Where is the locket?" Nimue screamed.

I looked into the crowd, who were all writhing on the floor, and spotted something shiny on the ground near a large, green, scaly monster. "Over there!"

Nimue went for it, but Hastur grabbed her and threw her into the stands above. Delilah and Cassandra cast spells on him, but he would not be kept for long, even with Rapunzel joining in.

I slid under the beam of light Baba cast and merged with the crowd. I reached for the glittering jewelry, but when I picked it up it was nothing but a ruddy pendant.

"Where is it?" I pushed the thrashing guests away as I searched the ground for the locket, but it was nowhere to be found.

That's when I saw a black silhouette, unmarred by the liquid acid, rushing for the front of the palace. The glimmer in its hands was unmistakable. It was the locket, and if the shadow made it out of the castle, then it would vanish into the ether.

"No!" I shouted, leaping over bodies. "Get them!"

But nobody else was in a position to help me. I was on my own. I sprang through the air and landed by the exit, but the shadow slid under me and kept running. I pressed out my palm and my own beam of light fired through the air, ripping a hole in the shadow. It dropped to the ground.

The locket rolled away. I grabbed it and turned to the great hall just as an explosion rocked the whole castle, flinging me backwards a dozen feet. Chunks of the castle rained down upon me. Every part of my body ached, and when I breathed in, the dust from the explosion filled my lungs. The castle was completely obliterated, nothing left behind but a brown crater.

Baba lay next to me, shattered wood embedded in her arm.

"Are you okay?" I asked.

"No," she shook her head. "I need about a week to recover, but I doubt we have the time.

"If you destroy that body, I will kill you."

I pushed a large piece of the castle brick off my pelvis and forced myself to stand. Something was surely broken, and the pain coursing through my body was unbearable, but there would be time for that later, too.

Nimue lay several yards away, with Lydia and Cassandra, each nursing injuries. In the center of the circle, the dust cleared to reveal Hastur.

"Is this how you want it? A final battle to show that my body reigns supreme?" His eyes were more filled with even bloodlust than usual. "Then we will make it a glorious battle and when I have won, I will bathe the world in your blood!"

He bent over, and when he rose, he was holding Rapunzel limp in his arms. With as much force as he could muster, he ripped the poor woman in half and sent the parts flying across the remains of the castle.

"That's not good," I said.

"Not at all," Baba said. "She was the strongest among us."

I held up the locket. "But she didn't have this."

"Then you are the one who must do the deed," Baba replied. "Press it into his heart, and then stake him with something long and sharp. It will be over. Then, we can fight over the rubble."

"I'm going to die if I fight him."

"Maybe, but we will be there, and maybe, just maybe we can beat him. Together."

"That sounds almost inspirational." I sneered. "I hate it."

"Distract him," Baba said. "And I will gather the others for a final assault."

I reached down and pulled a large stake out of my calf. It came from the foyer, a large wooden piece of that hateful mansion. It was perfect for a final stake in the heart of the King in Yellow.

I stepped forward, black blood pouring down my leg. "I have what you seek!"

Hastur wheeled around. "And what is that, my traitorous princess?"

I held up the locket. "Your heart, taken by Issha, before she betrayed her sister to give you eternal life. I offer it in return for your mercy."

Hastur laughed. "Even at the end, you think only of yourself. I have to respect that. Very well. If you give me the heart, I will spare your life, and even allow you to take part in the massacre of the infidels."

"I will enjoy that." I hobbled forward. "Did you know about the heart?"

He touched his chest. "I felt a hollowness inside of myself, but doesn't everyone? Once I destroy the heart, then I will never die."

I shook my head. "You can't do that. If your heart dies, you do, too."

"I see." He nodded, considering this. "Then thank you again, for I would have done the deed to myself."

We met in the middle of the crater. I looked at the side of my eyes to see the others ready for their final attack. They were waiting for my word, but if I could get him to take the heart himself, then I could end him myself.

"Give it to me."

I held out the locket and grabbed the stake tightly. "Gladly."

I dropped the locket but before it landed on his outstretched palm, he moved his hand away and it fell harmlessly to the ground.

Hastur's lips curled into a sinister smile. "You must think me stupid."

He lunged for me, and I ducked just as a half dozen of my sisters and allies fired on the dark lord. I snatched the locket as they peppered him with their magic. I spun around and punched, sending my fist with the locket through his body. I felt the locket latch on to his ribs, and he lurched forward, screaming.

I pulled back and then lunged forward with the stake. Hastur slammed his hand through my body at the same time that I stuck him through with the stake. He coughed, and then fell to the ground.

The blood didn't come immediately, but there was a

dribble, and then it gushed from my chest. I fell to my knees while my compatriots surrounded me.

"Bethel!" Nimue whimpered, putting her hands on me. "It will be okay."

The light went from my eyes, and I fell back. "Yes, it will be. Now."

I thought I would live forever, never doing a single good thing in my life, but I did. I did one good thing in my miserable life, and I died with a smile on my lips.

CHAPTER 61

RED

There was nothing left. No sign of the key and no way to make another one. All of that died with Shaun and his cryptic final words.

When he was made by the two, I gave them the power to control their destiny. If only they could take it.

I had no idea what that meant.

I tore the house upside down looking for a clue, any clue, and came away with nothing, except the location to the locked door that guarded the Dark Planet, and a collection of scribbled notes he'd left on his writing desk.

Maybe I could learn something from the papers. It was a long shot, but I had to try. If I couldn't figure this out, then everything, every little stupid thing that happened since I left the Fairy Realm, would be for naught. I decided to pocket the papers.

The Spindle returned me to the Celestial Realm, where I gave the attendant the coordinates to the door. They swallowed as they put them in, knowing where I was going, but they didn't argue with me.

I arrived on the planet next to a hundred-foot-high set

of red doors covered in vines and branches, like the forest had taken them for its own. Tall trees high blotted out the stars as I walked through the thatch and up the cracked stairs up to the massive doors. I pushed them as hard as I could, though I knew they wouldn't budge.

Each of the two doors had a story carved into it, filled with dragons, monsters, and gods, but neither one left clues on how to open the door. On the other side, the door was yoked to nothing but more foliage that had swallowed everything else whole. It was just like a fairy door; a portal into another world, another realm, outside of time and space.

I fell into the tall weeds and wept bitterly, like I had not ever wept in my memory. Everything I had done was fruitless. What a waste of a life. *Why was I given this gift only to fail in the end?*

I cried until I was out of tears, and then I cried some more. When I was done, I looked up at the magnificent ancient doors and stared, gathering my strength, ready to return to Rama and tell him of my failure. I hadn't accepted it, but at least I was resigned to it. I pushed myself up from the dirt, and I turned back to the Spindle.

A miraculous thing happened.

A loud, yawning creak cut through the air, and then the doors began to slide open. The light of a Dark Planet streamed toward me. *What had I done, except sit here and cry to make the door open?*

With a flash, a figure appeared. It was Nox, who smiled at me.

"Oh good," she replied. "Just in time. Now, come on. We have work to do."

EPILOGUE
NIMUE

It wasn't supposed to happen like this. I didn't know how it was supposed to go, but it wasn't supposed to end with Elvira, Bethel, and Rapunzel dead. It wasn't supposed to end with the castle destroyed, with Cassandra and Delilah barely able to stand, and with Lydia clinging to life after the final assault.

I dropped to my knees by Bethel and cried. "I'm so sorry. I should have protected you."

"There was nothing you could have done," Baba said, clothed in Elvira's radiant skin. "It was always going to end badly. At least the universe didn't end in the process."

"What do you know?" I replied. "You don't care about anything or anyone."

"That's not true," Baba said, but judging by the look on her face, she didn't believe it.

I looked over at Hastur. I pushed the hood from his head and found nothing but a decrepit skeleton underneath it, wearing a rusted crown. His magic had made him look formidable, but in the end, he was nothing. Like all powerful people—just a pile of bones, trying to pretend they matter to the universe.

I reached down and picked up the crown, tossing it to Baba. "There, our deal is done. Enjoy ruling over the ashes."

"Wait!" Cassandra said. "That wasn't the deal. We were supposed to rule together!"

"That's why we did this!" Delilah shrieked. "You lied to us!"

I shook my head. "You can rule with her if you choose, or you can fight about it. I rescind my claim. I'm done with this."

I pulled Rapunzel's nose from Hastur's cloak. She had done so much for this stupid thing, and now, when I had finally won it for her, she could not even use it. Ironic.

"I will not rule with others," Baba said.

"I don't care," I replied. "You wanted the crown, and I got it for you. The rest of it doesn't matter to me." I looked over at Delilah and Cassandra. "You can stay here, rebuild the rubble, or you can come with me. We can build our own kingdom somewhere else, far from the weight of Carcosa, where we can live a simple life."

A shock crashed through me, and Baba took a deep breath. "I don't know how simple it will be."

"What was that?" I asked, turning to her.

"The door back to the universe is open," she said. "The end is nigh."

AUTHOR'S NOTE

He's dead! There was a time in the middle of this whole book where I thought Hastur would make it to the twelfth book, but he's dead. He's dead. He's dead. Woooot!

If you liked Hastur, then I'm sorry for celebrating, but he literally was supposed to be dead two books ago, so I am very excited right now. Of course, if he died two books ago, I likely would have never made a place for Bethel in this book, and she was one of my favorite characters to write in the whole series. I absolutely loved how she was just nonplussed by even the most evil, terrible things that happened.

It's interesting, because I wasn't intending to mimic the arc of The Fairy Realm by having two different major storylines, with one resolving in book 3 and the second resolving in book 4, but it seems that has been engrained in me while writing this series.

Now, all my focus can turn to the Celestial Realm, and the impending doom brought on by the Primordials. If you follow my other work, you might be able to tell the very Lovecraftian inspiration for the Spore and the Primordials.

Heck, Hastur and Carcosa were a huge part of this arc, and they are just the tip of the Lovecraftian iceberg I have been trying to set up.

Even though there have been a lot of things I didn't expect for this latest installment, it's actually progressing pretty much how I planned on an overall scope. We were always supposed to go from the Dream Realm to the Fairy Realm to the Celestial Realm. I didn't expect the Underworld to come up, or the Dark Planet, but the major beats are all pretty much the same, and the train is still on the same track I planned out in 2018.

Wow, I have been working on this a long time, and writing these characters for many years. I really love them all, and this universe. I hope you do as well, and you're ready for the last book in this arc, *The Dark Planet*.

THE DARK PLANET PREVIEW
BOOK 12 OF THE OBSIDIAN SPINDLE SAGA

By:
Russell Nohelty

Edited by:
Leah Lederman

Proofread by:
Katrina Roets

Cover by:
JV Arts

Formatting by:
Turbo Kitten Industries

CHELLE

Rama sat in the middle of the shack that Kadlu brought us to through a series of poorly made tunnels running under the main city of her acid-rain torched world. I wasn't quite sure if we were under a major city or a minor one, but it didn't matter much. The sky had been torched in a battle between the gods, and the whole population was driven underground, so there probably weren't minor and major cities anymore, just ones that survived and ones that didn't. If the conditions of these people were any indication, it wasn't much of a victory to survive, but the people here still did it out of sheer stubbornness. I understood that. I lived, died, and came back again based on sheer stubbornness mixed with a hefty dash of spite.

Whether it was a major city or not didn't matter, in the end. It was the city closest to the Obsidian Spindle, which made it incredibly important to me. The Obsidian Spindle on Earth was closest to a rather inconsequential city... unless you happened to need transport to the Celestial Realm, or any of the myriad worlds that a Spindle could take you; a million miles traveled in a matter of seconds. *Being inconsequential was solely a matter of perspective.*

When I first entered the Dream Realm what felt like a hundred years ago, I thought the Obsidian Spindle situated behind the Emerald City was the most important object in the whole universe, unique in the cosmos to commune with the fates and return to Earth from the world of Urgu. I treated it with disproportionate level reverence and awe in those days, but I learned my lesson quickly; that there were thousands of Obsidian Spindles across the worlds of the universe.

When I became a fate myself after the death of Atropos, I found the truth; that the Obsidian Spindle was little more than a travel network set up by the gods to connect with other places in the universe so they didn't have to navigate space all alone, and to give them a way to triangulate around the universe so they didn't wind up missing a planet as it rotated around its nearest star.

The Obsidian Spindle was utilitarian, in the way a car, or a train was on Earth, and you wouldn't hold reverence for one of those unless you were an idiot.

If you were a god, traveling by Obsidian Spindle would be no more magical than taking a plane. Of course, in its way, a plane was one of the most magical things in the world. If you went back even a century, the thought of the average human being able to cut through the sky and reach from New York to London in a matter of hours instead of days or weeks would have been a fantasy akin to traveling between worlds. But now plane travel had become a mundane reality of our existence, just like the Obsidian Spindles had become to me. The only thing that retained its awe to me in the whole universe was Rose.

"Hey," Rose said as she caught my stare and walked coyly toward me. "Why are you looking at me like that?"

Rose had only been gifted with the god's magic for a short time, but she absolutely flourished when she became god-touched in a way that made me wonder if she needed me at all. We met when the both of us were poor and piteous, but now I remained that way and she had become a formidable force in the universe. All I was good for was getting captured, and putting her in danger, but she was a true steward of the universe, helping to bend it toward justice.

"Nothing," I said, shaking my head. "I just think that what you've done is amazing. You saved Rama, and—"

"Hey!" she shouted forcefully but politely. "We saved him together. Odin would have cut us down if you didn't come to rescue me."

"Maybe," I replied. "But I think you would have figured out a way out." I sighed. "That's just the way you are."

I never believed that the arc of history naturally bent toward justice. It took dogged determination by those with a strong will to grab the timeline of history and twist it to their whims. No, the arc of history listed to cruelty if anything, because the gods were cruel.

That was what I didn't understand until Kadlu told me about the true seat of power in the universe. A board of gods, called The Board by the uninspired gods that created everything in existence, had been entrusted with the day-to-day minutiae of running the universe, and had bent it to their whims; tilting the scales to favor the despots and strong men that they held in their own image. There could be no justice until the Board had been unseated from power...and that was not even our biggest problem.

No, that rested with the Spore.

Rose smiled at me. "Oh, so you're throwing yourself a pity party over here. I was wondering why you've been so distant."

"I'm not holding a—" I bit my tongue when I realized she was right. "Okay, maybe just a little pity party."

She placed her hand gently on my arm. "We saved each other enough that I thought we got over keeping score."

I dropped my head, unable to meet her eyes. "It's just— I really feel like a damsel that needs rescuing, and I hate that feeling."

She laughed. "Well, yeah, behind that kind of person sucks, but you're not that. After all, this whole craziness started with you saving me."

I sucked in a breath of air. "Yeah, but since then you've gotten blessed by two gods and all I've been able to do is die and get captured."

She grabbed my hands and squeezed them. "Wasn't it you who told me not to feel bad for not being the most powerful girl in the world—and that the only thing that mattered was what you thought of me?"

"Yeah," I said softly. "I guess so."

She laid her head on my shoulder. "And do you remember what you told me?"

I shook my head. "No."

I felt her smile even though I couldn't see it. "You told me that I was the most important in the world to you, and as long as that was true, and that you were the most important person in the world to me, then nothing else mattered. You told me that as long as that was true, we were the most powerful people in the whole universe."

I furrowed my brow. "Are you sure that's what I said. It sounds a little more cheeseball than I have the ability to be."

She shrugged as she pushed herself off my shoulder. "Maybe I'm editorialized a bit, but that was the gist. So, I ask you, Chelle, love of my life and light of my heart, am I still the most important person in the world to you?"

I squeezed her hand hard. "Of course. Always and forever."

"Good," she said with a small smile. "Because you are the most important person to me, which means that together, and that's all that matters in all of this."

I looked over at Kadlu. "I think your new friend would very much say saving the universe is the most important thing."

She smiled. "Without you, I would never have the courage to save the universe. All the strength I have, that I have ever had, is because of you." She looked over at Rama. "Now, I think Rama's ready to tell us what he knows. Are you going to come listen, or do you want to mope over here like a little baby?"

"Hey!" I shouted. "That was such a sweet moment and you ruined it."

She let my hands go and shrugged. "Tough love, baby. You gotta take the sugar with the salt."

I leaned forward and kissed her. "I take it all, forever. Now, come on. I think I'm done with my pity party. Let's go save the world."

RED

I spent so much time trying to find Nimue, and by extension the Dark Planet, that I never thought of what it would be like on the other side of the great locked door. The first thing I felt on the other side of the doorway was a gust of cold, bitter air. I had never smelt anything like the air in the Dark Planet. It reeked like the piteous cries of the tortured souls that screamed out for relief in the Underworld, and like the sweat that dripped off the condemned when all hope was lost and all that remained was doom.

The door opened into a thick forest where gnarled trees wove and braided their bark together to form a canopy that existed without leaves. When the forest finally broke into a field, I realized that even if there had been easy sight of the sky, there would not have been a star in the sky close enough to produce the light needed to create daylight. In fact, even as I strained my eyes to their limit, I could not make out one single light in the sky. I knew they called it the Dark Planet, but now I knew that the only things that could exist on it were the twisted, horrible creatures that thrived in the darkness.

"It is not all so bad as that," Nox said as she stared at the horror on my face. "Beauty grows in the darkness, too. That is what the gods you worship never understood. They only saw the beauty in the light."

"How is it possible for them to deny the darkness?" I asked, sitting in the field across from Nox, who had curled up in a tight cross-legged pose with her hands held tight against her knees. "I have been to the Celestial Realm, and there is barely a light in the sky. You would think they would honor the darkness as well as the light"

She shook her head. "There is so little you understand."

"Then explain it and quit treating me like a child. I may not understand, but I can learn."

"Very well." She took a deep breath, luxuriating in the harsh air that turned my stomach. "The first thing you must know is that the gods would never accept any light that burned brighter than themselves, and letting a star burn close enough to be felt dimmed their presence, or so their feeble brains believe."

"That much I understand, but that is not the whole story."

She shook her head. "No, it is not. The gods, or at least those you call gods, were not the first to rule the universe. Your Nox was not the first god of darkness. In fact, she was ridiculed when she chose to rule the darkness of the universe, but Nox knew the truth...that true power, true beauty, rested in the abyss." She held out her hand. "Without the darkness, the universe would be a millionth its size, just big enough to be crushed in my hand. Dark matter is everything, and yet they fear it, and by extension, humanity fears it."

"Then you must love the Celestial Realm."

"We did not call it that, when it was ours." She looked

out into the middle distance. "My people...they lived at the center of the universe once, where your Celestial Realm now resides. Even the gods could not deny its power after they kicked the rightful rulers of this place...once they banished us to the furthest reaches of the universe, a place outside of time and space, where they expected my brethren to die."

"But they did not die?" I asked.

"I hope not, but I truly do not know."

I took a deep breath. "And you have taken over Nox's body, but you are not her, right?"

"Correct. I am not the Nox you knew, though I retain her memories." The creature placed a smile on the god's face. "I am glad we can drop the charade. Those that know no better call me the Spore."

"Is she dead? Nox?"

The creature shook Nox's head. "Not quite. She can hear everything we are saying, but she is not, as they say on your planet, 'in the driver's seat'. We have lived in many gods, and Nox is easily the most difficult to control. Perhaps it is because she loves the dark as much as we do. I almost think we could have been friends, if our aims were aligned slightly better."

"Friends don't take over each other's bodies."

"Your friends, maybe," she said. "But yours is only one way of being, and it is not a very pleasant existence, truth be told. Where I am from, we live together, as one; individual, and together, as one. That is what we created this universe to be, but your gods had other plans."

"And you hope to bring your friends back from beyond the universe, and punish the gods for their insolence?"

"It is more than that." Nox looked over at me, but her eyes stared right through me. "Do you ever feel that this universe was not meant for you? Perhaps that you are fighting against a great truth. Perhaps that existence should not be so difficult as you make it out to be?"

"I do, but then, I am not from around here."

"No, you are not. You are special; a beautiful abomination, like me."

I sneered at her. "We are nothing alike. You aim to destroy the universe, and I work to save it."

"You are wrong." Her eyes went cold. "This universe is not yours to control. It was meant for my people, and it was taken from us. I am sorry that you have grown comfortable here, but you are parasites. The universe is dying, because you are not taking care of it, because you have no idea how to be good stewards of the life that we intended to thrive. Instead, you call it hideous, when it is truly the most beautiful thing in existence, made in the image of the gods that wanted them to rule the universe, not you. The only reason you continue to thrive in this place is because the gods fight against entropy to keep it so. You, and the gods that made you, are parasites, and I aim to exterminate you for the good of the universe."

"I'm not going to allow you to destroy the universe, even if you think you're trying to save it."

Nox smiled. "That is what I like most about you, human. You refuse to go quiet into oblivion. If you were not so important, I would show you the truth right now, but..."

She trailed off, and my face turned sour. "What does that mean?"

Nox took a deep breath as she stood. "This is how the universe should smell. I am happy that at least one place was able to find the equilibrium we intended."

I stood up as she brushed herself off. "You didn't answer my question."

"Enough, parasite," she snapped. "You know what you must in order to fulfill your purpose, and you only know what I told you because it would be cruel to send you to what is coming with you knowing a small morsel of the truth."

"You say that like I will help you."

She smiled an unnatural smile. "You will, whether you want to or not, but now you must make a choice. Come with me willingly to gather what I need from this place and face your nemesis head on, or fight me here and now, learn how futile it is to fight your betters, and lose what little agency I have given you."

I snarled, but then I bit my lip. Nox was powerful, and this being controlling her must be even more so in order to bend her to the being's will. I needed to bide my time, feign complicity, and wait for my moment to strike.

"You speak of Nimue," I said. "She is the nemesis I seek."

"I do."

"If you aim to bring me to Nimue, then I will come with you, as long as you allow me to kill her without interference."

"It amused me that you think to bargain with me, but fear not, I will not interfere with your heart's desire. You have my word on that, for what that is worth to you."

I stepped forward. "Then I will come with you, for now."

"You have made a wise choice." She held out her hand for me to grab. "The other way would have been less than pleasant."

ARIEL

I knew something bad had happened before I even opened my eyes, because when I tried to pull my arms to wipe the sleep from them, I found myself bound tight enough that I had no range of motion in any of my extremities. When my eyes fluttered open, I found myself in a sterile, circular room with three tables in the center of it.

A large, silver, blinking box stood on the far end of the room, with different colored ropes from red to green to blue to purple snaking from it across the room to each of the metal beds. I craned my neck up to see a large dome overhead with a hole in the center where a large rod poked through into the dark, starry sky.

"You're up," a hoarse voice whispered to me.

I turned my head to see Hypnos bound next to me, his arms and legs splayed and wrapped with thick leather against a circular slab of polished metal. I didn't know something so basic could hold a god, but he was captured by Nox, and—

Suddenly, the last days came flooding back to me. Traveling to the Nightmare Realm to find Rapunzel's eye, traveling to a dark castle on a high mountain, being saved by—and then returning to the Dream Realm to find those I promised protection in Hypnos's bosom slaughtered—dusted by Nox, a wild look in her eye, and an unconscious Hypnos crumpled at her side. I wasn't sure if he was dead or alive, but now I knew the truth, and in the crushing pain of so much death, it made my heart flutter in excitement.

"You're alive!" I shouted. "Praise the gods."

Hypnos shook his head, a bitter look on his face. The normal pink of his eyes was no longer there, replaced by a dull brown. "Don't praise my brethren. They are not to thank for my salvation."

"Very true," a voice chimed in as a door slid open next to us. A god wearing a shimmering blue medallion, every hair on his head white and kissed by the finest silk walked into the room. His eyes were black as ink and so was his tongue. "My mistress sends her regards. She hoped to meet you when you returned, but she has been called away on pressing business, so you were left in my care."

"And who are you?" I asked.

"You may call me Ukko, I suppose. However, that is merely my corporeal body. My kind do not like names, but you call us the Spore. Even saying that name tastes bitter on this one's tongue. You may call me Ukko, or Spore, or nothing, though I prefer the latter."

"Ukko was one on the Board," Hypnos said. "I recognize that name, and his face."

He looked down at his hands. "Yes, this body was a member of the Board. It satisfied our needs for a time, but recent development has forced us to change tactics."

"Wait," I replied, a raging pain in my forehead. "The Board? What is that? I have never heard of such a thing during all my time in the Dream Realm."

"Because you are not in the Dream Realm," Hypnos growled. "You have been rendered corporeal by my mother's dark magic, no doubt as some part of her devious, diabolical plan."

Not in the Dream Realm? Corporeal? That meant I had a body, and had been rendered back unto the universe for the first time in three hundred years. I sniffed the air and it felt sweet compared to the bland nothing that I had smelled since my soul had been resurrected in the Dream Realm. *Could such a miracle be true?*

"I don't understand. How?"

Ukko smiled. "It is old magic, for sure, from when my kind ruled the world, but I assure you it's quite possible, if banal, magic. When my kin ruled the universe, it was very common. Everything, in its way, is energy made corporeal. It just hasn't been seen in many generations because the gods have bastardized our powers."

"What are you talking about?" I ask

"Of course, you are only human, which means you have feeble minds." Ukko looked at Hypnos. "Do you want to tell her, since you created them?"

"I suppose I'll do it, if only so you'll shut up." Hypnos sighed. "Several billion years ago, the universe was created in a flurry of energy by the Primordials. They are older than time itself, and when they grew tired of an endless eternity filled with nothingness, they turned to a new project, creating a universe they could mold to their wills. Eventually, in their dabbling, they created the first gods, who birthed more and more."

"It was one of our worst ideas," Ukko cringed, bile in his voice. "For soon enough their vanity got the better of them, and they decided they should be in charge. We were more powerful, but they were numerous, like viruses, and they pushed my kin back to the edge of the universe, and bound them from it."

I looked over at Hypnos. "Is that true?"

He nodded. "It's true. They wanted to turn existence into—" His face twisted in a way that I had never seen, filled with anger and contempt. "—We did not agree with their twisted view of the universe."

"It was our universe to twist to our wills!" Ukko shouted, before calming down. "That is the vanity I meant, and it still courses through your veins, but no bother. Time is nothing to us, and in short order we will make things right that were once put wrong."

A kernel of understanding blinked onto my face, and then vanished. When I couldn't quite piece it together, Hypnos growled at Ukko. "They aim to open the barrier that exists between us and then, and take back what we took from them, bringing forth an era or horror on this universe that you cannot even imagine."

I did not like the sound of that one bit. "No. You can't."

"Yes, we can do anything, that is the point." Ukko smiled an odd smile. "You cannot stop us. Far from it."

"I can try." I tried to wriggle unsuccessfully from the restraints.

"You will fail, but you are welcome to try. Perhaps you might even stall us for a moment, but then you will take your place in our grand plan."

"I want no part to play in your sick games," I spat at him.

"That is not your choice, of course. You will help usher in a new age whether you like to or not, and then, the universe will be ours."

ALSO BY RUSSELL NOHELTY

The Obsidian Spindle Saga

The Godsverse Chronicles

Ichabod Jones: Monster Hunter

Cthulhu is Hard to Spell

My Father Didn't Kill Himself

Sorry for Existing

Gumshoes: The Case of Madison's Father

The Invasion Saga

The Vessel

Worst Thing in the Universe

The Void Calls Us Home

The Marked Ones

The Little Bird and the Little Worm

Gherkin Boy

Find a complete list at

https://www.russellnohelty.com/books/

About the Author

Russell Nohelty is a USA Today bestselling author, publisher, and speaker. He is the author of dozens of novels and graphic novels including The Godsverse Chronicles, The Obsidian Spindle Saga, and Ichabad Jones: Monster Hunter. He has a very entertaining newsletter, which you can join at www.russellnohelty.com. He lives in Los Angeles with his wife and dogs.

Get one of my favorite books for free at:
    www.russellnohelty.com/mail
    Substack:
    https://authorstack.substack.com
    Bookbub:
    https://www.bookbub.com/profile/russell-nohelty